LOCH

An ancient legend guards a deadly treasure.

When former Navy SEALs turned treasure hunters Dane Maddock and Bones Bonebrake discover a sunken German U-boat at the bottom of the Irish Sea, they find something shocking. The tooth of a prehistoric reptile embedded in the hull! Soon, Maddock and Bones join a beautiful reporter and an eccentric cryptid hunter on an action-packed search for a lost treasure and brings them face to face with one of the world's most enduring mysteries.

PRAISE FOR DAVID WOOD
AND THE DANE MADDOCK ADVENTURES

"David Wood has done it again. Within seconds of opening the book, I was hooked. Intrigue, suspense,monsters, and treasure hunters. What more could you want? David's knocked it out of the park with this one!"-Nick Thacker- author of The Enigma Strain

"A page-turning yarn ' blending high action, Biblical speculation, ancient secrets, and nasty creatures. Indiana Jones better watch his back!" Jeremy Robinson, author of SecondWorld

"Dane and Bones.... Together they're unstoppable. Rip roaring action from start to finish. Wit and humor throughout. Just one question - how soon until the next one? Because I can't wait." Graham Brown, author of Shadows of the Midnight Sun

LOCH

A DANE MADDOCK ADVENTURE
DAVID WOOD

Loch, A Dane Maddock Adventure

Published by Adrenaline Press
www.adrenaline.press
Adrenaline Press is an imprint of Gryphonwood Press
www.gryphonwoodpress.com

Cover by Kent Holloway Book Cover Design

Edited by Melissa Bowersock

This book is a work of fiction. All events, locations, and characters depicted are products of the author's imagination or are used fictitiously.

ISBN-10: 1-940095-69-7
ISBN-13: 978-1-940095-69-1

BOOKS BY DAVID WOOD

THE DANE MADDOCK ADVENTURES
Dourado
Cibola
Quest
Icefall
Buccaneer
Atlantis
Ark
Xibalba
Loch

DANE AND BONES ORIGINS
Freedom
Hell Ship
Splashdown
Dead Ice
Liberty
Electra
Amber
Justice
Treasure of the Dead

JADE IHARA ADVENTURES (WITH SEAN ELLIS)
Oracle
Changeling

BONES BONEBRAKE ADVENTURES
Primitive
The Book of Bones

JAKE CROWLEY ADVENTURES (WITH ALAN BAXTER)
Blood Codex
Anubis Key

BROCK STONE ADVENTURES
Arena of Souls
Track of the Beast (forthcoming)

MYRMIDON FILES (WITH SEAN ELLIS)
Destiny
Mystic

STAND-ALONE NOVELS
Into the Woods (with David S. Wood)
The Zombie-Driven Life
You Suck
Callsign: Queen (with Jeremy Robinson)
Dark Rite (with Alan Baxter)
Primordial (with Alan Baxter)

DAVID WOOD WRITING AS DAVID DEBORD

THE ABSENT GODS TRILOGY
The Silver Serpent
Keeper of the Mists
The Gates of Iron

The Impostor Prince (with Ryan A. Span)
Neptune's Key

PROLOGUE

April 30, 1918
The Irish Sea

"Officer on deck!" The men inside the control room of the UB-85 came to attention and snapped precise salutes at the sublieutenant's sharp command.

"Carry on." Captain Günther Krech moved a few paces into the room and halted, looking around at the cramped space.

With quick replies of, "Aye, Sir," the men returned to work.

Inside the periscope well, Sublieutanant Lars Westmann turned back to the periscope and peered into it. He scanned back and forth, and then again, and again, until Krech suspected the man was stalling.

"Do you see any targets out there, Oberleutnant?" Krech asked.

Now, Westmann turned to face him.

"Nothing yet, Kapitänleutnant. We just surfaced."

Krech nodded, unable to hide his grimace. They needed prizes, and needed them soon.

The North Channel of the Irish Sea, less than twenty kilometers wide, had long been a favorite site for buccaneers seeking to prey on shipping between Ireland and the main British isle. Now, in the midst of the Great War, a new threat patrolled these waters.

The U-boat, German's greatest weapon against the might of the British navy, had made these waters deadlier than ever. Just this month, U-boats had sunk nearly 280,000 tons of Allied shipping, gaining much-needed supplies.

Krech's boat had sunk none, her full complement of ten torpedoes still waiting to be unleashed. That needed to change.

Westmann approached slowly, casting nervous glances from side to side. Sensing his second in command sought a private audience, Krech moved out of the control room. With the roar of the UB-85s engines to contend with, he didn't have to go far in order to be out of earshot of his crew.

"Permission to speak, Kapitänleutnant?" Westmann asked, his voice hoarse and his brow lined with worry.

Krech nodded. He already knew what the man was going to say.

"We have been out here for two weeks, and have met with no success. We can't stay much longer."

"I am aware of that. We have time, still."

"Precious little." Westmann cleared his throat. "The prize the agent gave you yesterday, if it is as valuable as you believe, surely that will suffice?"

Krech shook his head. "It's more complicated than that. We must take at least one prize before we return." He stared down at Westmann until the underliuetanant nodded. "Take her up top and we'll have a look."

Krech stood atop the conning tower, peering out at the moonlit horizon through a pair of binoculars. Down below, Westmann, flanked by two junior officers, stood on the deck, also searching for targets.

The early morning breeze tugged at Krech's uniform. The sea gently rocked the ship. Dawn was not far off. Surely he'd soon see the telltale column of smoke that announced a ship's approach.

Without warning, a loud crash pierced the quiet morning. It rocked UB-85, sending the crewmen tumbling to the deck. Krech managed to remain standing, looking all around to see what they had hit. His first thought was an iceberg, but that made no sense. It was the wrong place and wrong time of the year for such an obstacle.

"What did we hit?" he shouted.

As if in reply, another crash shook the boat.

And then he saw it.

A dark hump sliced through the water, circling away from UB-85, then changed directions. Krech watched as it shot forward, impossibly fast, once again on a collision course with the boat.

"It's going to ram us!" he called, moments before the third collision, the hardest yet, sent him tumbling to the deck.

"Is it a whale?" one of the officers cried.

"I don't know what it is," Westmann replied. "But we can't take many more of those collisions." He took out his sidearm and the other two followed suit.

Kneeling atop the conning tower, Krech pressed his binoculars to his face and searched for the creature. He spotted it, thirty meters away, turning for another run. Could it be a whale? The dark hump rising from the water looked wrong. And then, for the briefest of seconds, the creature raised its head.

Krech's binoculars slipped from limp fingers and clattered to the deck. Everything the agent had told him came rushing back.

"It's true," he whispered. "He wasn't lying."

Against the crackle of small arms fire, the creature smashed into the ship again. The impact sent the sailors flying. And then the deck tilted wildly to starboard as the monster flung its massive bulk up onto the deck.

Clouds had drifted across the face of the moon. Krech could make out few details in the darkness. He heard a loud, metallic wrenching, and fired his sidearm in the direction of the sound. In the brief, faint light of muzzle flashes, he caught a glimpse of dark skin and the mangled remains of UB-85's gun mount.

"This beast might sink us," he whispered. He had to make sure the treasure was safe.

For a brief, irrational second, he wondered if he could return the treasure to the creature. But that was absurd.

But is it any more absurd than the guardian of the treasure following us out into the open sea?

He could ponder the improbability of it all after it was over, if they lived through it. Right now, he had to get down below.

His crewmen had regained their feet and emptied

their pistols into the massive beast. Krech did the same.

The creature, whatever it was, let out a reptilian hiss and slid its bulk back into the water.

"Do you think it's gone?" Westmann asked.

"I don't know," Krech said. "We should get out of here. Come on."

He slid down into the hatch, followed by the other officers. All around, sailors cast confused glances in his direction.

"Kapitänleutnant," Westmann called, "the hatch will not close."

"What do you mean?"

"That…thing damaged it. We can't dive."

Krech's guts twisted into an icy knot. "And unless we can repair it, we'll take on water in anything other than the smoothest seas."

"Kapitänleutnant, what is happening out there?" one of the midshipmen shouted.

Before Krech could reply, something tore through the fabric of the hull. He had a moment to register the sight of shiny, black fangs penetrating the steel skin of UB-85 and then water began streaming in. The men shouted in surprise, and then the beast bit into the ship again, this time ripping long narrow gouges in the steel.

We are all going to die.

With his crew's cries of alarm ringing in his ears, Krech turned and ran for his quarters. They might not survive this night, but he would preserve the treasure.

CHAPTER 1

Off the Coast of Wigtownshire, Scotland

Gray clouds rolled in across the dark waters of the Irish Sea. Dane Maddock looked out at them, his guts twisting in a knot. The last thing they needed was another fruitless day of treasure hunting cut short by the inclement Scottish weather. It had been a risk taking on a job so far from home, but it had seemed like the right thing to do at the time. He had a lot on his mind, and getting away from familiar places, and a few familiar people, had been too enticing an opportunity to pass up.

"Key West this place is not." Bones Bonebrake folded his powerful arms over his chest and scowled at the dark horizon. "At least you won't get sunburned, mister short, blonde, and pale."

Maddock eyed the tall, deeply-tanned Cherokee. "When have you ever known me to sunburn, mister Coppertone?"

"Mister Coppertone! I like that." Bones flashed a smile, but it quickly turned to a frown. "Wait a minute? Is that racist? I never know what I'm supposed to be offended by nowadays. I think I'm supposed to hate the Washington Redskins and that stupid 'tomahawk chop' that the Braves and Seminoles fans like to do."

In the years since they'd served together in the Navy SEALs, Maddock had mostly grown accustomed to his friend's cavalier attitude toward the sensibilities of his own race. Still, sometimes Bones managed to make him cringe.

Maddock grimaced. "Can we save that conversation for later? I'd like to get in one more dive—a quick in and out in case the storm doesn't change direction."

"I suppose. You sure you don't want to knock off early? I want to try some real Scotch." He gazed pointedly in the direction of the Scottish mainland. Bones' lack of enthusiasm at the prospect of another dive underscored just how badly things had gone thus far. Ordinarily, Maddock couldn't keep him out of the water.

"As soon as Matt and Willis get back, we'll go in."

No sooner had Maddock spoken than a pair of heads broke the surface. Willis Sanders and Matt Barnaby swam to the side of *Sea Foam* and hauled themselves on board. Willis was another former SEAL comrade, while Matt was an ex-Army Ranger.

"Man, I ain't seeing a thing down there." Willis, a dark-skinned, muscular man of almost a height with Bones, mopped the salt water off of his shaved head. "I hate to say it, but I think we might have come here for nothing."

"Maybe," Matt said, running a hand through his short, brown hair. "But even if the wreck of the *Regal Crown* isn't down there, there are bound to be other wrecks waiting to be discovered. This place has seen centuries upon centuries of ship traffic. I think it might be worth expanding our grid and seeing what else might be down there."

"Sure, take Maddock's side." Bones glanced at Willis. "Notice how the white people all stick together?"

"Hey, I'm on *your* side!" Corey Dean, the fifth member of the crew, called from the cabin. "I'm totally ready to pack it in for the day."

"Gingers are a minority, too," Willis replied.

"Bones and I are going to make one more run at it before the storm hits," Maddock said. "We'll take Matt's advice and expand our search. We'll head northeast and broaden the search parameters beyond our current grid."

Bones frowned. "You want to go against the current? Seems like we ought to do the opposite."

Maddock shrugged. "Our current grid is based on a projection of how far the *Regal Crown* would have drifted since its sinking. Maybe we overestimated the distance." The *Regal Crown* was a British ship reputed to have gone down in this area in the late eighteenth century. Rumor had it there were gold and jewels belonging to a noble house on board. It had never been found.

"You mean, maybe *I* overestimated it?" Corey asked, once again poking his head through the cabin door.

"Yes, but I wasn't going to say so." Ignoring Corey's profane reply, Maddock fixed his mask and regulator in place, sat down on the deck rail, and flipped backward into the water. His tensions eased as he plunged into the welcome depths. A splash in his peripheral vision moments later told him Bones was right on his tail.

Enveloped by the cool water, they swam hard against the weak current. It wasn't long before they had passed beyond their marked search area. He knew they shouldn't go too far afield. Time was short and to venture out too far would be an unnecessary risk. Maddock gave Bones the signal, and they dived.

This stretch of seabed looked no different than any other section they had explored that day. Maddock swam at a steady clip, sweeping the beam of his headlamp back and forth. The circle of light roamed over sand, rock, and vegetation, but nothing of interest. They continued on, staring balefully down at their relentlessly ordinary surroundings until Maddock was ready to call it a day. He was about to turn back when Bones caught his attention and pointed off to their right.

Swimming in the direction Bones indicated, the two men soon found themselves looking down into a crevasse. At first, Maddock saw little of interest, but then he realized that what he'd initially taken for gray stone was, in fact, metal. As they drew closer, Maddock recognized it for what it was—the conning tower of a German U-boat. A spark of excitement flared inside of him. He doubted it would hold any treasure, but the history buff in him couldn't resist taking a closer look.

They swam along the length of the submarine, taking in its well-preserved lines. Maddock could clearly make out the deck gun, conning tower, and the periscope, all encrusted in a century of marine growth. It was a UB, a World War I German submarine. He'd never seen one in person and was fascinated by it.

He spotted a jagged gash in the starboard side, wide enough for a diver to swim through. Heading down for a closer look, Maddock was puzzled to see a series of smaller cuts, scrapes, and indentations all around the tear. Some were punctures, almost as if something had bitten through the hull. Of course, that was impossible. He wondered what sort of weapon would leave such oddly shaped holes.

He tried to form a mental image of the submarine's last minutes. Probably it had surfaced for some reason and come under fire from a surface vessel. The punctures must be the result of machine gun bullets. But what had caused it to sink? Not such small arms fire, to be sure. A larger shell must have struck the submarine, causing it to take on water. The scrapes and the large tear in the side would have likely been caused by the rocky side of the crevasse as the dying boat slid down to its final resting place.

He glanced at his dive watch. They hadn't been down very long and had plenty of air left, but he had no idea what the weather on the surface was like. He glanced at Bones.

As was often the case, his friend knew exactly what Maddock was thinking. Bones nodded and then pointed emphatically at the hole in the sub. The message was clear—*let's check this thing out.*

They swam slowly, careful not to stir up too much silt, which would cause virtual whiteout conditions, rendering them near blind.

As they moved forward, he marveled at the many sights he'd seen only in photographs. Inside the control room, a myriad of handles, like steering wheels, jutted out from the walls. He spotted a pair of gauges, and carefully wiped the grime from their surfaces. One measured depth, the other, fuel. Nearby, a small manhole afforded access to the periscope well.

Bones spotted the voice pipe. Predictably, he removed his regulator and began mouthing words into the trumpet-like end, sending up a stream of bubbles.

Laughing internally, Maddock made a circular gesture to tell his friend they needed to hurry up and finish their exploration before it got too late. They didn't want to run out of air down here.

They passed through the electrical control room, the engine room, and into the torpedo room. Oddly, the sub appeared to still be fully armed. The attack that sank it must have come suddenly for the sub not to have fired any of her deadliest weapons.

They completed their exploration, picking up a few artifacts—coins and the like—but nothing of great value. Bones paused on the way out and gave the sub's damaged hull a close inspection. Maddock wondered what had drawn his friend's interest, but when he swam closer, Bones turned and waved him away.

When they returned to their boat, the *Sea Foam*, Maddock was relieved to see that the storm had, indeed, changed directions. The sun was setting to the west, and the first hint of evening's approach was painted purple on the eastern horizon, but the clouds had fled, leaving behind clear skies and balmy seas.

"Y'all find anything good down there? You were gone a while," Willis said.

Maddock recounted the discovery of the U-boat and showed them the items he'd collected.

"It was cool," he finished, "but I can't say we found anything of much interest."

"Oh, I don't know about that." Smiling, Bones reached into his dive bag, took out something large and dark, and held it out for the others to see.

"What in the hell," Willis marveled, "is that?"

CHAPTER 2

Ben MacDui, Scotland

"You know you don't have to go up the mountain this way?" Isla Mulheron paused and looked ahead at the faint path that skirted a steep cliff as it wound upward toward the summit of Ben MacDui. To the north, low-hanging clouds shrouded the mountaintops in mist. A stiff breeze ran through her long, auburn hair, sending a chill down her spine as she imagined invisible hands nudging her closer to the edge. She set her jaw, stiffened her resolve, and followed along behind her interview subject.

"This way will be of much more interest to your readers. You should get some pictures for the magazine." "Grizzly" Don Grant turned and struck a pose—hands on hips, one foot propped on a boulder, face tilted slightly upward.

Isla sighed. "Fine. Can you try to look more... natural?"

Grizzly's brow creased. "What do you mean? Like this?" He moved a hand to his chin and attempted a "Thinker" pose.

"Tell you what," Isla said, focusing her camera on him with the greatest reluctance. "Just start climbing the trail. Our readers like 'action' photos."

"But you won't be able to get my face," he protested.

"It'll be all right. I'll take plenty of photos when we reach the summit." The American cryptozoologist was handsome, with wavy brown hair, penetrating eyes, and stubble that emphasized his strong jawline, but his personality ruined it. "Maybe you'll fall over the cliff," Isla whispered as Grizzly began his ascent, dropping down to all fours and splaying out his hands and feet to make the climb appear more difficult. Ever the professional, she chose the best angle to support the illusion, focused, and snapped several photos.

"How does this look?" he shouted back over his shoulder.

"Brilliant!" She gave him a thumbs-up. "But you can get up and walk now. I've got plenty of you pretending to…I mean, scaling the rock."

Grizzly flashed an approving smile, scrambled back to his feet, and resumed the trek up the mountainside.

Isla snapped a couple more pictures, just to prove the buffoon was capable of walking upright, and then followed along. Not for the first time, she questioned the life choices that had brought her to work for *Scottish Adventure* magazine. Granted, it paid better than her job in New York, and her flat here was twice the size of what she could afford in The Big Apple, but the subject matter upon which she was expected to report ranged from boring to downright insulting. This one was the latter.

"Up ahead is where the trail forks off. We'll be crossing the Allt Clach nan Taillear." Grizzly somehow managed to botch almost every syllable of the name. "The way ahead is rough and thick with boulders, but it will give the reader a more authentic adventuring experience. Lots of photo-ops, too. I just hope you can handle it." He gave her a sly wink.

Isla managed a smile. With greater effort, she kept both hands closed in fists, despite the fact that her middle fingers were struggling to rise. She heard her nan's voice in her head.

Failing means you're playing.

At least the man was trying, if trying badly. Somehow, despite his apparent lack of skill, he'd managed to fashion a career and a bit of a reputation, even if it was among conspiracy theorists and nutters.

"I'll be okay. I did a fair spot of climbing when I lived in the States."

"You lived in America? I thought your accent was milder than the locals," Grizzly said, scrambling up the trail.

He wasn't wrong about that. In America, Isla had

found her thick Scottish accent often worked against her, and she'd worked hard to lose it.

"Where have you climbed?" Grizzly asked.

"Mostly in the Adirondacks. I did some climbing at Yosemite last summer."

"Have you ever summited Everest?"

Isla stopped short. "No. Have you?" Perhaps she'd missed something in the man's bio. The Everest angle would improve the story dramatically. Maybe there was more to him than she'd initially believed.

"Not yet," Grizzly said. "I had an offer from a television show last year. They wanted to look for the Yeti. I turned them down. They weren't willing to meet my appearance fee."

Isla highly doubted that, considering *Scottish Adventure* was paying him nothing at all. In fact, he'd only gotten in touch with the magazine after his request for coverage had been turned down by several larger media outlets. *He's all bum and parsley,* she thought. It would be a miracle if the man gave her anything of value for her column. Yet, her editor would hold her to blame if her column were lacking.

Up ahead, Grizzly paused and turned to face her. She winced as his over-laden backpack swung out over the edge of the cliff. "The boulder field is up...whoa!" Like a cartoon character, Grizzly windmilled his arms as he overbalanced and began tipping backward.

Isla dashed forward and managed to grab him by the belt as he fell. She pulled with all her might, hauling the sturdily built man back from certain death. He fell forward, and they landed in a heap on the rocky mountainside and slid several meters before skidding to a halt. She found herself lying, winded, on her back, with Grizzly on top of her.

"Well, that was an adventure, wasn't it?" He grinned down at her.

Isla would have punched him, but she was busy trying to catch her breath.

Grizzly stood, folded his arms, and quirked an

eyebrow as he looked down at her. "Panic attack," he said, sagely. "Just relax. Most women have them at altitude. It will pass in a minute."

Isla couldn't help herself. She lashed out and kicked Grizzly square in the shin.

"Ow!" He staggered back two steps before kneeling and rubbing his shin. "I know you're scared but don't take it out on me. I was only trying to help."

Isla finally managed to suck in a breath. The air was thin here, close to the summit of the second-highest peak in Britain, and it took several lungs full before the dizziness subsided. By then, she'd managed to suppress her urge to push the American over the cliff. He offered his hand, and she debated for a full second before taking it and letting him help her to her feet.

"Like I said, you'll be all right." He turned and headed toward the boulder field. "Watch your step near the cliff," he said. "I wouldn't want you to fall."

This time, Isla's middle finger won the battle of wills.

"Lord, just get me through this assignment."

CHAPTER 3

Off the Coast of Wigtownshire

Maddock looked at the dark, curved object in Bones' hand. He recognized it immediately, and a shiver ran down his spine. "That is one big tooth."

"Let me see." Willis took the tooth from Bones and held it up for closer inspection. It was long, slightly curved and roughly cylindrical in shape, tapering to a point at one end. "Looks like a shiny, dark gray carrot." He passed it over to Matt.

"If it's a shark tooth," Matt said, turning it over in his hands, "it's a variety I've never seen before."

"That's no shark tooth," Maddock said. "But I have no idea what it actually is."

"I think I can tell you exactly where this thing came from." Bones grinned broadly, excitement evident in his twinkling brown eyes. In his usual, infuriating manner, he kept his silence.

Corey broke first. "Fine, I'll bite. What do you think it is?"

Bones took the tooth from Matt and held it up. "Before I say anything, I need you guys to keep an open mind about this and hear me out."

His words elicited a chorus of groans from the crew. Matt buried his face in his hands, and Corey gazed wearily up at the heavens.

"Here we go again," Corey muttered.

"Aw, man," Willis grumbled. "Is this another one of your cryptids?"

"Screw you guys." Bones glared at each man in turn until they fell silent and he once again had their undivided attention. "I read a story about a World War I-era German U-boat that went down somewhere west of Scotland. The thing is, it wasn't attacked, at least, not by the enemy. Some sort of sea creature took it down."

"What sort of creature?" Maddock asked, already

doubting his friend's story.

"No one knows. There aren't any surviving accounts of what it looked like—only the fact that it was able to bite through the hull of the sub. It took whole chunks out of it."

"Sounds like it would make an excellent B-movie," Matt said. "Are you sure this isn't something you saw while you were drunk?"

Bones scowled at him.

"I hate to say it," Maddock began, "but I think the story could be true. We saw puncture holes in the sub that I first thought might have been made by bullets, but they didn't look quite right. Considering their shape, they could easily have been made by teeth like this one."

Willis ran a hand over his head, sweat glistening on his bare scalp. "But I've never heard of anything that can bite through the skin of a sub."

"It happened," Bones said. "The one thing we know for certain is I found this thing," he brandished the tooth, "stuck in the side of the U-boat. Whatever this creature is, it had a powerful bite."

Silence fell over the crew as they considered this new bit of information. A thought occurred to Maddock, though it pained him to share it with the others.

"I'll bet some of the ancient sea creatures had a bite that powerful."

"Like dinosaurs?" Matt asked.

Maddock nodded. "Yes, but then again, that sub went down about a century ago."

Corey pursed his lips and frowned at the tooth in Bones' hand. "What if, and I know this is far-fetched, someone did this as a prank? They found the sunken U-boat, came back later and shoved a stolen fossil into one of the bullet holes."

Maddock shook his head. "What would be the point? There'd be no telling how long that sub would go undiscovered. Besides, that tooth is clearly not fossilized."

"Now you're catching on." Bones patted Maddock

on the shoulder. "I'll make a monster hunter out of you yet."

"Hold on. Y'all saying there's sea monsters in this channel?" Willis' eyes darted back and forth, as if something deadly lurked nearby, ready to rise up out of the water and snatch him.

"I didn't say 'sea monster,'" Maddock said. "All I'm saying is something strange might have happened here about a hundred years ago."

"That's nice," Matt said, "but I'm guessing this tooth would only bring us bad publicity if word got out that we found it. We don't need that."

"But we can't just let it go," Bones pleaded. "Come on. It's not impossible that something survived. We've seen strange things before. If there are still some prehistoric sea creatures swimming around, I want to prove it."

Willis shook his head. "Don't even start that talk about Nessie. I've been listening to that crap from you since the first damn day of SEAL training."

Matt chuckled. "SEAL training must be as easy as they say if Bones can manage to chat about cryptids the whole time." The former Army Ranger seldom missed an opportunity to needle the crew's three ex-SEALs.

Willis rolled his eyes. "Man, I will rip your arm off and beat you with it."

"Promises, promises," Matt said, then turned his attention back to Bones. "You can't still believe in Nessie. I mean, come on. That surgeon guy admitted he faked his photograph. It was all over the news."

"He lied," Bones said flatly. Nessie was a touchy subject for the big Cherokee.

"Why would he do that?" Matt asked.

"To protect the creature, or creatures, actually. He knew the Nessie legends were true and he felt guilty about all the attention he brought to the loch. He probably thought he was doing the right thing by recanting his story."

"While you guys debate monsters," Corey said, "I'm

going to do a little research. Maybe I can get some idea of what sort of creature this came from." He took the tooth from Bones and headed back into the cabin.

"Whatever. This has been a fun diversion," Matt said, "but we need to return to the reason we came here in the first place—treasure. I doubt there's profit in finding one mysterious tooth. So, what's our next move?"

"We make another run at the U-boat," Bones said.

"What for?" Willis asked. "The tooth is cool, but we got to get paid."

"Oh, did I forget to tell you?" Bones' eyes widened, and he gaped in mock surprise. "There's another part to the story. The U-boat was rumored to be carrying a stolen Scottish treasure."

CHAPTER 4

The summit of Ben MacDui

Isla kicked at a patch of snow that stubbornly held on against the approach of springtime. Patches of green poked up through the many gray rocks and boulders that cluttered the summit of Ben MacDui. It was chilly up here, but she'd known what to expect and had dressed accordingly. Grizzly, it seemed, was not as well prepared. He shivered, stamped his feet, and paced to and fro. Trying to tune him out for a moment, she turned away and gazed out at the hilltops and peaks, some still speckled with snow, that encircled the mountain on which they stood. It was a beautiful sight, calming, but not sufficient to soothe her growing annoyance as Grizzly began to give orders.

"You should get some pictures of me from over there," he pointed to his left. "I'll look better from that side."

"Couldn't you just turn?" she asked, once again taking out her camera.

Grizzly seemed to think she was kidding. He stood shivering, hands thrust in his pockets, until she repositioned herself on his good side.

"Don't you have anything in your pack you could put on to keep you warm? Some gloves, a few layers of clothing, maybe?"

"I do," Grizzly said, "but layers make me look fat. I'll put them on after you take your pictures."

"In that case, let's get it done in a hurry." She focused and began clicking away. Meanwhile, Grizzly launched into a lecture about Ben MacDui.

"Standing at a height of just over thirteen hundred meters, that's over four thousand feet to us Yanks," he winked at the camera, "Ben MacDui is the tallest peak in the Cairngorms, and the second-highest mountain in England after Ben Nevis."

"You mean in the United Kingdom," Isla corrected.

"What's that you say?" Grizzly asked.

"We're in Scotland, not England. Ben Macdui is the second highest mountain in the United Kingdom."

Grizzly smiled. "Ah, I understand the confusion. England is part of the United Kingdom, and Scotland is part of England, so it's really all the same. Now, let's get back to it. I'm cold."

Isla grimaced and raised the camera. "Bawbag," she muttered.

Grizzly finally turned and picked his way across the mountaintop, over to the summit indicator. Isla kept clicking the shutter, hoping he might take a spill.

The summit indicator was a stone disc set upon a pedestal atop a large cairn. All around it, arrows pointed to various hills and mountains, with their names and distances marked. The legend at the center denoted its purpose and dedicated it to the memory of an Alexander Copland.

Grizzly struck a pose and resumed his lecture.

"Here atop MacDuffs's Hill, the summit indicator was set in place in 1925 by…"

"Hold on," Isla said. "You do realize this is not a video camera?" She held her camera out for emphasis. "It's not recording anything you say."

Understanding crept across Grizzly's face like the slow approach of dawn.

"Okay. Don't you have a recorder or something?"

Isla took a deep breath, counted to five, and let it out in a huff. "I think I've got enough photos for now. How about you put on some warm clothes, and we find a place out of the wind to do the interview segment? Behind one of those, maybe?" She pointed to one of the many horseshoe-shaped stone walls that dotted the mountain's summit.

"Are you sure you want to sit there? Some say the Grey Man built those." Grizzly winked and waggled his eyebrows.

"I think the World War Two commandos who built

them during training would disagree with you."

A glint of intelligence flashed in Grizzly's eyes. He tilted his head and looked at her suspiciously. "You know a lot about this place, don't you?"

"I studied up on it in preparation for our interview." That was true, though hardly the whole story.

Grizzly stared for a long moment, but if he doubted her, he didn't say so. He opened his pack, donned a few extra layers of clothing, and then took out a tent which he proceeded to pitch on the leeward side of one of the stone bivouacs.

Meanwhile, Isla busied herself studying the summit indicator. She snapped photos of every inch of its surface, from every angle. After that, she stood and simply gazed at it, as if something of value would leap out at her.

"What are you doing over there?" Grizzly called.

"Nothing." She whirled around at the sound of his voice. Pain shot up her leg as her foot caught between two stones and her ankle twisted. She fell hard, cracking her knee and scraping her palms on the rocky ground.

"Hold on, I've got you." Ignoring her protests, Grizzly ran over to her, helped her to her feet, and supported her weight as they made their way over to the tent.

She hated accepting help from this buffoon, but he seemed to know about ankle sprains. He cautioned her not to remove her hiking boot, explaining that, should she take it off, the foot might swell, making it impossible to put the boot back on. He tightened her laces, propped her foot on his backpack, and laid a cold pack from his first aid kit atop her swelling ankle.

"RICE," he said. "Rest, ice, compression, elevation."

This display of competence, however limited, gave her hope that the article might not be entirely without merit. Maybe she could pluck some valuable nuggets from the dross he spewed forth.

"As long as I'm resting my ankle, we might as well talk about the Grey Man. I just hope we don't miss him while we're sitting in here," she kidded.

"Don't worry about that. He's seldom seen any time other than dawn. That'll be our best chance to catch sight of him."

"I didn't know we were spending the night. I'd have brought my own tent."

"The tent is for you," Grizzly said. "I'll be outside in my sleeping bag. I don't expect the star of the show to appear during the night, but I want to be ready if he does."

His words put Isla at ease. She took out her notebook and recorder, shifted into a comfortable position, and began the interview. "Why don't you start by telling our readers about the legendary Grey Man?"

As Grizzly launched into his description of the cryptid, his entire countenance changed. No longer was he a puffed-up phony, preening for the camera. He was knowledgeable, sincere, even earnest at times as he held forth on the subject.

Am Fear Liath Mòr, Scottish Gaelic for The Big Grey Man or The Auld Grey Man, was a mysterious cryptid known to haunt the summit of Ben Macdui. Most reported sightings were not sightings at all, but climbers hearing its footsteps crunching the gravel as it stalked them. Those who caught a glimpse of the creature described the Grey Man as thin, covered in dark fur, and standing anywhere from six feet tall to three times the height of a man. Some believed it to be a Yeti-type creature while others considered it more of a supernatural being. All, however, agreed that its presence induced terror in those who encountered it.

"There have been many accounts from reliable sources, such as professors, naturalists, and experienced mountaineers. Some think it's merely a legend, but time will tell." Grizzly lapsed into a reverential silence.

"You really believe this stuff, don't you?" Isla asked.

"I believe in possibilities," Grizzly said. "I don't just take it for granted that all legends are bogus. I know at least some of them are real."

"How do you know that?"

Grizzly pursed his lips, considering. "Personal reasons. I don't really like to talk about it."

That surprised Isla. She'd figured there was nothing Grizzly wouldn't want to talk about. The man hadn't shut up since the moment they'd met, but now he seemed lost in his thoughts.

Suddenly, as if waking from a dream, he gave his head a quick shake. "I'm going to set up outside. There's food and water in the pack. Call me if you need anything." He picked up his sleeping bag and headed for the door. "I'll come and get you if I see anything. Otherwise, I'll wake you before sunrise. Fingers crossed that we'll see something remarkable."

When he was gone, Isla turned to a blank page in her notebook and began writing her article. She preferred longhand for the first draft. Her thoughts and words seemed to meld better that way. She decided to focus on the mountain itself: its history and its stark beauty. The hunt for the Grey Man would merely be the framework for a meatier piece designed to entice tourists to visit this lonely mountain.

An hour later, her work complete, she allowed her thoughts to drift to the summit marker and the inscriptions on the top. Nothing had stood out as being unusual. She wished she were home right now, cross referencing her notes with the high-resolution photographs she had taken. There *had* to be something there. The latest clue seemed genuine.

After thirty minutes of fruitless pondering, she accepted that she'd make no breakthroughs by merely thinking about it. She had no appetite, but still took a few minutes to dine abstemiously on granola, nuts, and dried fruit. With no service on her phone and nothing else to do, she decided to call it an evening. A couple of ibuprofen washed down with water, and then she was curled up in her sleeping bag, trying to clear her mind.

The alarm on her phone went off far too early. With only the greatest reluctance, she slipped from the warmth of her sleeping bag and into the chilly air inside the tent. There was no sign of Grizzly or his sleeping bag. Apparently, he'd held to his pledge to remain outside during the night. Her opinion of the man slightly improved, she put on her coat and gloves and crawled out of the tent.

She found the cryptid hunter sitting on his sleeping bag in between the tent and the shelter of the rock wall. He held a steaming cup in his gloved hands and gazed toward the east, where the first streak of gray painted the horizon.

"Is that coffee?" she whispered.

"It's only instant," he said. "You can have some if you like." He inclined his head toward a thermos and a tin cup.

Isla helped herself to a cup of the bitter liquid. Oddly, she occasionally enjoyed a cup of instant coffee. It brought back childhood memories of camping trips with her father, sitting around the campfire, listening to him spin tales of Celtic mythology.

"Did you light a fire?" she asked.

"Wing stove and a sierra cup," he said. "The flame is tiny, so we don't have to worry about scaring away the Grey Man."

Isla didn't know what either of the items he listed was, but she didn't really care. She was just happy to have some coffee.

"How's your ankle?" he asked.

"Better. I barely feel a twinge when I put my weight on it."

Grizzly nodded. "When we leave, we'll take the easy way down, just to be safe."

"Thanks for that."

They sat quietly, drinking coffee and watching the sun rise. She found herself thinking that this would be a romantic moment were she with someone other than Grizzly. At least she'd reached a point at which she could tolerate the man. In fact, the silence they shared was almost companionable. On the downside, dawn was breaking and, as expected, they'd caught no sight of the Grey Man.

At least I won't have to rewrite the ending of my story, she thought.

Grizzly stood, stretched, and yawned. He suddenly stood ramrod straight. "Oh my God!" He grabbed her by the shoulder. "Look over there!"

"If you're trying to wind me up, it won't work." Isla turned and looked in the direction he indicated. Her breath caught in her throat.

In the midst of the morning fog, at the western edge of the summit, stood a tall, wraithlike figure.

"Am Fear Liath Mòr," Grizzly whispered. "The Grey Man!"

CHAPTER 5

Off the Coast of Wigtownshire

Maddock rose early and followed the aroma of freshly-brewed coffee up to the main cabin, where Corey was already at work.

"You do realize I'm not paying you by the hour," he said, taking a seat at his friend's side.

Corey grinned. "This isn't work. At least, not really. Just researching sea monsters."

"You forgot to close the tab with tentacle porn on it." Maddock tapped the screen.

"Just a pop-up window," Corey said, hurriedly closing one of the browser windows. "Searching for terms like Leviathan, Kraken, and giant squid turns up some weird stuff." His crimson cheeks and reddening ears told a different story.

"Gotcha," Maddock said. "Find anything interesting?"

"Not yet, still in the information gathering stage. I've steered clear of the obvious up to this point. At least, obvious for this part of the world."

"Plesiosaur?" Maddock asked, naming the creature most frequently associated with the Loch Ness phenomenon.

Corey nodded. "I'll dig into that later."

"Sounds good. Once the guys are awake, we'll start working on the strongbox we brought up from the sub."

Their final dive of the previous day, one in which Matt and Willis had joined Bones and Maddock, hadn't turned up any treasure. They'd found a few more coins, as well as some buttons and knives that might be of modest value to collectors. The item of most interest had been a strongbox found in the captain's quarters. Given its weight, Maddock doubted it held any sort of treasure, but he'd thought it worth the effort of retrieving. Today they'd open it and see what was inside.

He busied himself with calisthenics, then enjoyed another cup of coffee as he watched the sun rise. He thought about calling Angel, his fiancée and Bones' sister. She was in Los Angeles, meeting with an agent who wanted to capitalize on her growing fame as an MMA fighter and turn her into a movie star. What time was it there? Late night?

"Oh, what the hell." He punched up her number. After a long pause, it began ringing. No answer. Either she was asleep or otherwise occupied. He'd check in with her later. Of course, he wasn't sure she would be eager to take his call. Things had been tense between them the past few weeks. He couldn't put a finger on it, but something was different.

"I hate it when you navel-gaze." As if from nowhere, Bones appeared at his side, holding two steaming mugs. "Thought you might like a refill."

"Thanks." Maddock accepted the cup. "And you know I hate it when you sneak up on me like that."

"I'm not sneaking. Indians just now how to move quietly, unlike white people, who can't do anything without waking the neighbors."

"Fair enough." Maddock took a sip of coffee, trying to decide if he wanted to broach the topic of Angel. "Bones, has Angel said anything to you lately?"

"She says all kinds of stuff to me. Mostly 'assclown' and 'asshat.' She really likes to work 'ass' into things. No pun intended."

"You know what I mean."

Bones shook his head. "Bro, you know my rule. I stay out of your romantic crap. She's my sister, you're basically my brother, and incest is for rednecks, and you know how I feel about them."

"So you don't know of any reason things might have changed between us? She says we're good, but something feels off." He hesitated. "I saw a press photo of her at some movie premiere, and she wasn't wearing her ring."

"Dude, sometimes I don't know which one of you is the girl in your relationship. Actually, I do." Bones grinned, but his smile evaporated when he saw the look in Maddock's eyes. "Okay, fine. She hasn't said a freaking thing to me, but I have a theory. You and I are never going to stop doing what we do. At least, not as long as we're able. Angel's the same way. She's got a lot of new stuff going on in her life. Maybe right now is not a good time for the two of you to be more than friends with benefits."

Maddock nodded. It made sense. For most of the time he and Angel had known one another, he'd been the more accomplished of the two. Now, she was a prominent fighter in mixed martial arts, and her beauty had brought her a degree of celebrity and a plethora of business opportunities. And, it seemed, Hollywood fame might not be far behind.

"Then again," Bones said, "I'm an advocate for the friend with benefits arrangement, so I'm biased."

Maddock forced a smile. "Food for thought." He drained his cup, stood, and sucked in a breath of fresh morning air. "I think I've explored my feminine side enough for one day. Let's wake the others and see what's inside the strongbox."

Belowdecks of the *Sea Foam*, Maddock and crew had set aside a special room for the care and preservation of artifacts. Different items required various types of treatment, depending on composition and the setting in which they were found, and this room was equipped to handle just about any set of circumstances they might encounter.

The strongbox was locked, but the real challenge was the years of pressure and sea water that had effectively sealed it closed. It took Maddock a full two hours to carefully work it open. He could have cut through it, but the meticulous nature of the task afforded him the opportunity to lose himself in the work and forget his troubles.

While he attended to the task, the others worked on the rest of their finds: cleaning and preserving the coins and artifacts recovered from the sub. They all paused to watch when Maddock opened the box.

His heart sank when he removed the lid and saw that, as he had feared, the sea had managed to penetrate the closed box. Bit by bit, he scooped out the salt water, filtering it to make sure he didn't lose anything. Finally, when the water level was almost at the bottom of the box, he got a good look at its contents: a tarnished pocket watch; several gold coins; a rectangular box about the size of a paperback novel; and a piece of black stone.

"I'll bet this box belonged to the U-boat captain and these were his personal effects," Maddock said, carefully lifting the watch out and passing it over to Matt.

Next, he removed one of the gold coins. The obverse side featured the profile of a bearded man and the words *Friedrich Deutscher Kaiser Konig V. Preussen,* while the reverse displayed the German imperial eagle.

Maddock held the coin up and read aloud, "Deutches Reich 1888. Twenty mark. "

"That'll be good for gas money," Willis said, helping Maddock move the coins to another container.

"What's up with that rock in there?" Bones asked. "It's not an uncut gemstone, is it?"

"Hardly." Maddock picked it up and examined it in the light. About the size of a golf ball, it was black, smooth and glossy on three sides, and rough on the other. "It's obviously a corner piece broken off a larger stone."

"The captain, or whoever, valued it enough to lock it in the strongbox. Wonder why?" Bones asked.

"I don't know. I see some lines carved in it, but not enough to tell if they were part of some text, or maybe an image or design. We'll definitely hang on to it, though."

The smaller box was sealed even tighter than the strongbox, and Maddock had no choice but to use main force to cut it open. Moisture had penetrated this box too, though not as thoroughly as it had the strongbox. Inside lay a journal. The pages were sodden, but the book had at least held together.

"Anything cool inside?" Bones asked.

"Not sure." Maddock laid it out on the table and, using a pair of rubber coated tweezers, opened it. He let out a small groan. The writing was smeared so badly that he could make out only inky squiggles. After the first few pages, the next several clung together and would not be parted. Not ready to give up just yet, he turned it over and worked his way backward, again using the tweezers to turn the blank pages until he came to the final entry. This one was legible. He knew only a limited amount of German, but one word, which was the same in English, stood out.

Monster!

CHAPTER 6

The summit of Ben MacDui

The tall, gray figure stood motionless in the swirling mist, making no move to come closer. It was thin, impossibly so, with disproportionately long legs, and around its head shone a halo-like glow. Perhaps it was the cold morning, the fog, or the surreal nature of the encounter, but Isla began to shiver.

Calm down, she told herself. *You have a job to do.* Quickly, she took aim and began snapping photographs.

"You are getting all of this, aren't you?" Grizzly asked.

"Absolutely."

"Great. I'm going to try to capture it on video." Grizzly leaned down and rummaged around in his backpack.

Just then the creature hunched down and began to slowly amble forward. Isla sucked in her breath.

"It's coming," she whispered.

"Really?" Grizzly stood, holding up his video camera.

The creature stood, raised its arms, and froze.

Isla stared, trying to comprehend this odd behavior. A creeping suspicion filled her mind. And then it struck her.

"I think I know what this is." Still snapping pictures, she rose to stand beside Grizzly. As she stood, another dark figure suddenly appeared.

The cryptid hunter gasped. "There's another one! I can't believe this. No one has ever seen two Grey Men before. I'm going to try and get closer."

"Don't bother," Isla said.

Grizzly ignored her. He stepped over the low stone wall and, still filming, approached the two shadowy figures. As he moved toward the shadowy Grey Men, one of the figures also began to move forward, as if in lockstep with him. Grizzly froze.

"I think we should remain still," he said. "They don't seem to want to move unless we move first."

Isla let out an exhausted groan. She lowered her camera, rubbed her eyes. "That's because they are us."

"What are you talking about?"

"It's a Brocken Spectre."

"A spectre?" Grizzly asked, still pointing his camera at the figures. "They're ghosts?"

Isla pressed her fingers to her temples, feeling a headache coming on. "You're kidding me, right?"

Grizzly slowly lowered his video camera and turned to face her. "Let's pretend I don't know what this Glockenschpectre is and you explain it to me."

"In a nutshell, a Brocken Spectre is a shadow cast in fog. It requires a very specific set of circumstances—sufficient fog plus the proper angle and amount of light. Sunlight, moonlight, even a flashlight can create the illusion. That's why the image appears so long and thin. It's a distant shadow."

"And that's why it seemed to move when I did."

"Correct. The second image showed up when I stood." She sighed. "I read about them ages ago, but the memory didn't come back to me until I actually saw the phenomenon in person."

"So it's just a shadow," Grizzly said.

"Exactly. See how they're already vanishing as the sun grows brighter?"

Grizzly nodded. "And the glow around the head must be sunlight refracted by the water vapor in the air."

"It's called a 'solar glory.'"

Grizzly continued to stare at the faint images until the rising sun melted them away.

Despite her misgivings about the man, Isla couldn't help but feel sympathy. He was an optimist, open to possibilities that she was far too cynical to even consider. Isla knew all too well how it felt to have your illusions shattered.

"I'm sorry," she said, and meant it.

Grizzly turned, rubbing his hands together and

smiling. "Sorry about what? We just proved the Grey Man is real!"

She held up a hand. "Wait. We did just observe the same phenomenon? You heard my explanation."

"Sure I did, but we solved the mystery! We proved that the sightings weren't just figments of someone's imagination. All right, it's not Bigfoot's cousin, but the witnesses actually saw something, and now we know what it was. I call that a win."

Isla was surprised to find herself agreeing with Grizzly. They *had* just solved an enduring mystery. More accurately, she had solved it. Conspiracy theorists and cryptid hunters around the world wouldn't thank them for it, but that was all right with her. That was one demographic whose readership she didn't crave.

"Do you mind if I quote you on that?" It was probably the wisest thing he'd said since they'd met.

"Not at all." Grizzly's eyes were alight with triumph. "I pitched this idea to Jo Slater, and she said it would be a waste of her time."

Where had Isla heard that name before? "Isn't she on television?"

"She hosts *Expedition Adventure*. The new season's delayed, something about a personal tragedy, but she's apparently getting ready to start up again. I can't wait until she sees the video!"

"I'm glad you're happy."

Grizzly shrugged. "I'm not usually an 'I told you so' guy, but I heard through the grapevine that she's been calling me 'vapid' and 'unprofessional.' This will show her."

Isla reflected on the turn of events. Maybe their success, relative though it might be, boded well for another mystery she hoped to solve. One it seemed she'd been trying to unlock her entire life.

As they broke camp, Grizzly shared his concluding thoughts about the Grey Man. He opined that the hikers who reported hearing the sound of being followed were probably hearing echoes of their own footsteps. He concluded by saying their discovery felt bittersweet.

"I'm happy that we know the truth, but I'd really like to find a cryptid some day. An actual, living creature."

"What's next for you?" Isla asked.

"I think you already know," Grizzly said, slipping into the straps of his backpack and buckling it above his hips.

"Actually, no. I only researched Ben Macdui and the Grey Man. I didn't study up on any of your other projects."

Grizzly folded his arms and gazed down at her, a condescending smile painting his lips. "Come on. We've only known each other a day, but aren't we past playing games? I'm not blind, you know."

Isla rolled her eyes. "You're the one playing games here, and I really don't have time for it. If you don't want to tell me about your next project, that's fine. I won't include it in the article." She turned on her heel and strode away.

"You think I didn't notice how much attention you were paying to the summit indicator?" Grizzly called.

His words stopped her in her tracks. He couldn't possibly know, could he? "I took pictures," she said through gritted teeth. "That's my job."

"Yes, you did." The sound of crunching gravel marked his approach as he strolled over to where she stood. "Dozens and dozens of close-up images of every inch of its surface. Those will look great in the magazine."

"I thought they would look interesting."

Grizzly narrowed his eyes, his smile vanishing. "You thought it would lead you to the treasure of the Tuatha de Dannan."

CHAPTER 7

Off the Coast of Wigtownshire

Silence hung in the room as everyone stared at the journal Maddock held in his hands. *Monster.* He'd have to translate the entire entry just to be certain, but this, combined with the tooth they'd found embedded in the U-boat, appeared to confirm what had sounded like a far-fetched tale when Bones told it. Of course, that was true for most of his stories.

"Can you read all that?" Willis asked.

"A bit of it. My German is rusty."

"Let me take a look." Bones moved to Maddock's side and squinted down at the words formed in a neat hand.

"Come on," Matt said. "You speak German?"

"I took it in high school. A bit more in junior college, then some in the Navy." Bones shrugged, his attention on the book.

"Why German?" Matt prodded. "Wouldn't Spanish be more practical?"

Bones turned a long, level look at his friend. "You've known me all these years, and you don't know the answer to that question?"

Matt flipped his hand in a "go on" gesture and raised his eyebrows.

"The French hate the Germans, and you know what I always say."

"Screw the French," the others chorused, chuckling as they spoke.

"Amen, brothers. Now, let's take a look at this thing."

It took some time, but Bones, with help from Maddock and an online German translation program, managed to decipher the text. It was what Maddock had expected, and a little bit more. Just as they had finished,

Corey appeared, carrying a manila folder. He joined them as they all circled around and read it together.

30 April, 1918

I write these words fearing that I and my men are doomed. The curse has followed us. As night fell, something began slamming against our hull, powerful crashes that shook the very framework of our boat but no enemy vessels were in sight. And then, with a terrible shriek, something breached our hull in several places at once. We thought it might be enemy fire, but as we fought to stem the flow of sea water into the ship, it happened again. I saw it with my own eyes—razor sharp fangs, terrible to behold. I did not believe our agent when he handed me this small portion of what he insists is a valuable treasure, nor when he told me of the beast that guarded it. Has this same monster come to reclaim its prize, or is this one of its brethren? How is either one even possible? Does it want this small bit of treasure back, or is it merely punishing us for the damage done to something it holds sacred? I regret that I will not be able to show this to the Kaiser. It would bring great shame to the Tommies to realize they have been sitting on a false throne.

After they'd all finished reading, Willis was the first to break the silence. "Man, I don't know about messing with no monsters, but I do like the sound of treasure." He rubbed his hands together and smiled.

"But there is no treasure on that sub," Matt said. "We searched that thing from stem to stern."

"No, I mean the treasure he's talking about in this journal," Willis said.

Maddock nodded. "If this captain's account can be trusted, a German spy found something of great value. Whatever it was, he couldn't bring it all with him, so he took just a bit of it. Whatever it was, it apparently would have embarrassed the British for it to surface."

"And the monster that guarded it got pissed off and came after him," Bones finished. "I don't see what's so hard to believe about that."

Maddock chuckled. "It would be harder to believe if we hadn't seen the tooth and the bite marks for ourselves."

"Something else is bothering me," Matt said. "There were no bodies on the U-boat. What happened to them?"

"According to the legend," Bones said, "the creature damaged the sub, but broke off its attack when ships from the Royal Navy arrived on the scene. The Germans knew they were sinking, so they ended up surrendering."

"And the captain didn't want the British to get their hands on his treasure," Maddock said.

"You think there's anything in here that might help?" Willis pointed at the journal. "I know the front part was unreadable, but if some of the later entries are legible, they might mention where he went and what he did."

"Let's see." Maddock began turning the pages again, working from back to front, but almost immediately he met with disappointment. The previous page contained only a few legible words. The page before that, only two. Four more pages back, the journal was the same inky sludge as the front of the book.

"Dead end," Matt said dully.

"We'll have to get creative," Maddock said. For some reason, he still felt they could solve this mystery. It wasn't like they'd never tackled something like this before. "The sea monster attack is such a far-fetched legend that I'll bet no one's ever taken a serious look at it. Maybe, with some research, we could learn more about the captain and his crew."

"You mean if I and maybe Jimmy do some research," Corey said. Corey was a computer whiz, and their friend Jimmy Letson was an absolute legend.

"Do you really need to ask?" Maddock said. "But that's not the only angle. If we can figure out what this treasure was, we could hunt it on our own. It won't be as quick as if we had a journal entry saying, 'dig here,' but that doesn't mean it's impossible. We're good at finding treasure."

"Yes, we are," Willis agreed.

"Do you think the black stone could be a piece of this so-called treasure?" Bones asked. "The journal mentions 'damaging something sacred.' You wouldn't phrase it that way if you found a treasure chest and snagged a handful of gold and jewels."

"And the bit of stone appears to have been chipped off of something larger." Maddock scratched his chin. "Whatever this treasure was, he had to leave it behind, but it was significant enough, maybe unusual enough, that he wanted the Kaiser to know about it. What's more he wanted to be believed."

"If this treasure is just a big, black chunk of rock, I'm not sure there's going to be money in it," Willis said. "Don't get me wrong, Maddock, I'm curious about this stuff too, but I got to get my mama out of Michigan and set her up down in Florida with the rest of us."

"I understand." Disappointment welled inside Maddock. There was little he enjoyed more than unraveling a historical mystery, but he owed it to his crew to take care of them. They'd done all right the past few years, but none of them were exactly well-off. He owed it to them to remain here and keep searching for the colonial-era shipwreck. He glanced at Bones. The big Cherokee was turning the black chunk of stone over and over in his hands, a glum expression painting his face.

Corey cleared his throat. "If you two want to stop acting like a couple of emo kids, I think I've got a solution."

"What's that?" Maddock asked, absently flipping through the ruined journal.

"You and Bones can head off on one of your legend quests, or whatever the hell you call it. Meanwhile, the real treasure hunters will stay here and bring up the gold on the colonial-era ship I just found." He held up the manila folder he'd brought along.

Maddock dropped tweezers and gaped at Corey. "Are you serious?"

Corey nodded. "While you all were screwing around down here, I worked a new grid in the direction you suggested. I found it right away. Even sent UMA down to check it out." UMA was a remotely-controlled underwater camera they often used for scouting out wrecks. "I liked what I saw."

Maddock's heart raced. "What did you find?"

"See for yourself." Corey opened the manila folder to reveal a high-resolution printout of an underwater photograph. At the center lay a broken chest, its brass bands discolored but still easy to make out, and spilling out of it…

"Gold!" Bones exclaimed. "Hell yes, you did it, you ugly, ginger virgin!" He high-fived Corey, who seemed to be trying to decide whether to smile at the praise or protest the unfair characterization.

"Do you guys think you can take it from here?" Maddock asked Willis and Matt. "The gold is just lying there waiting to be scooped up, but if anyone can screw this up…"

"It would be Bones," Matt said. "So get him out of here as soon as possible. We'll keep you posted on how the dive is going."

"We might even save a little gold for you." Willis winked.

"That settles that." Maddock turned to Bones, who couldn't hide his excitement. If there was one thing Bones loved more than a dive, it was hunting cryptids.

"I know how we should start," he said.

"How's that?"

Bones held up the tooth. "See if we can find out where this thing originally came from."

CHAPTER 8

Old Mill Inn, Pitlochry, Scotland

Isla was impressed with Grizzly's choice of the Old Mill Inn as the site of what she was already thinking of as their "negotiation." Located in Pitlochry, south of Ben Macdui, the inn boasted quality dining as well as luxurious accommodations. She still wasn't convinced she wanted to work with the man. In fact, she was kicking herself for even giving him the time of day. He'd made a fool of himself at times during their sojourn at the mountain, but he'd somehow managed to graduate from dunderhead to numpty in her mind. In any case, he'd assured her he was going after the Tuatha de Dannan treasure whether she joined him or not, so perhaps she ought to work with him for no other reason than to try and keep him in check.

"What are you going to have?" he asked, peering over his menu at her.

"Chicken killiecrankie," she said, closing the menu.

"What, exactly, is that?"

"Chicken stuffed with haggis and served with a mash of roasted roots."

Grizzly cocked his head. "You actually eat haggis?"

Isla laughed. "Only joking. I don't eat that stuff unless my nan makes it, and even then, it's only out of a sense of obligation. I'm having the Caesar salad."

"Good call. I'm all about the rib eye. I hear Scottish beef is top-notch."

"I'm not much of a meat-eater, but my dad always swore by it. Of course, I don't think he ever ate beef from any other part of the world, so his opinion might not be worth all that much."

They made small talk for a while, enjoying bottles of Dark Island Reserve, a popular Scottish ale, and enjoying the placid atmosphere of the inn. As she sipped the strong drink, enjoying its rich, malt flavor, Isla learned a few interesting things about Grizzly.

The youngest of three children, his father had died when he was sixteen. His older siblings, already out of university, or "college," as he termed it, and trying to get started in their own lives and careers, were no help to his mother. Mentally unstable at the best of times, the death of her husband plunged her into a deep depression, one from which she never fully covered. She lost her job and spent the next several years getting fired from various hourly-wage jobs. Thus, it fell to Grizzly to make sure the bills were paid.

He worked night and weekend jobs until he finished high school. He was a mediocre student, except for biological sciences, at which he excelled. One of his high school teachers helped him obtain an entry-level position at a nearby zoo, where he took advantage of their tuition reimbursement program to eventually earn his degree. None of this, however, impressed his mother or his siblings.

His brothers, both white collar workers in the corporate world, took pleasure in winding him up about his job shoveling piles of dung. His mother never acknowledged his role in keeping the mortgage paid and caring for her, particularly during her lowest periods. She criticized and belittled him at every turn.

"All I had were the animals and my books about cryptids," he said, without a trace of self-pity. "I guess I was so dissatisfied with my everyday life that it made me want to believe in anything that would make the world a bigger place, full of greater possibilities than what we know."

"That was science fiction for me," Isla said, hating the fact that she was finding any common ground with the annoying American. She also knew the pain that came from losing one's parents.

"Sci-fi depressed me," Grizzly said, taking a swig of Dark Island. "I enjoyed the stories, but knowing I'd never get to see any of the other planets in the universe and know for sure that something else was out there really bummed me out."

Isla frowned, then remembered that the American idiom "bummed" meant "depressed." It had nothing to do with one's backside.

"You couldn't visit other planets, but you could cross the globe looking for strange creatures."

"Exactly."

"What happened with your mother? Did your brothers finally step up and take responsibility?"

Grizzly laughed. "Hardly. Mom took her own life right after I finished college."

Isla sucked in a breath through her teeth. "I'm so sorry."

"It was a long time ago." He made a small, dismissive wave, and then barked a rueful laugh. "Would you believe, all that time, Mom had been sitting on all kinds of stocks and bonds passed down from my grandfather? She could have covered all our bills without either of us working. I guess that's why she never appreciated my efforts—they weren't actually needed."

Sympathy flooded through Isla followed by a wave of remorse at the way she'd treated the man. "That's not exactly true, you know. It doesn't sound like your mum was in any state of mind to use the resources she had."

Grizzly nodded thoughtfully. "It all worked out in the end. I managed to sell off the stocks and cash in the bonds without my brothers ever finding out. I pretended I was too grief-stricken over Mom's death to care what happened to the house and what little was in it. I walked away from it all while they sold everything for what little they could get and split the proceeds, cutting me out of course. I know what I did was unethical, illegal even, but it allowed me to start my career as a cryptid hunter. Besides, my brothers never lifted a finger for me or Mom, so I think inheriting her house and car was far more than they deserved." He drained his ale and let out a tiny belch that he didn't bother to cover.

You had to go and spoil it, Isla thought. Still, she had gained a new perspective on the man. He was still far too full of himself, but she could at least understand how he'd turned out that way. Generosity had brought him nothing but pain and rejection, while his first real act of selfishness had set him free. The question was, knowing this about the man, could she trust him to work with her and not double-cross her?

Their meals arrived, and as they dined, they finally broached the subject they'd danced around thus far.

"All right, let's talk about the Tuatha de Dannan," Isla said. "Do you believe in a supernatural race that dwells in the Otherworld?" She held her breath, waiting for his reply.

Grizzly considered the question for a few seconds before giving a quick shake of his head. "I don't believe in a literal Tuatha, but I believe in the four treasures that bear their name."

"The four jewels?" she asked.

"No. I believe the word 'jewels' is used figuratively to express just how precious these treasures are. The actual treasures are: the Spear of Lug, against which no army could stand; the Sword of Nuada, a glowing sword that, when drawn, none could resist; the Cauldron of Dagda, from which no one came away unsatisfied; and the Stone of Fai."

"Which would cry out beneath the king when he claimed sovereignty," Isla finished.

"So, we're on the same page," he said.

"It appears so. We have the same understanding of what the treasure truly is, and we apparently agree that it's not in Ireland, despite the historical associations between the Irish and the Tuatha."

"Belief in the Tuatha isn't a purely Irish phenomenon," Grizzly said. "And the Lia Fáil stone on the Hill of Tara is not the Stone of Fai, no matter what some say."

"Agreed," Isla said. Her own ancestors hailed from Ireland, so she thought she had a good perspective on the subject. That, and the fact that the myths, legends, and treasures of the Tuatha were a family obsession—

one she'd never been able to shake. She pushed her half-finished salad away and sat up straight. "How does a cryptozoologist find himself on the trail of the Tuatha treasures?"

"According to some legends, the treasure is guarded by water kelpies. That's what drew my attention to the mystery, but I'm definitely in this for the treasure hunting aspect." He steepled his fingers and leaned forward, all business. "Now that I've solved the Grey Man enigma, I'll have some added credibility."

Isla cleared her throat and quirked an eyebrow. "Who solved it?"

"Sorry. Now that we, mostly you, solved the mystery."

She smirked and gave a small nod to indicate he could continue.

"I guarantee you I can pitch this to Jo Slater and she'll bite. Well, almost definitely. She's an unpredictable sort. Even if she doesn't, I've got enough connections to finance a documentary crew and turn this into a television special."

Isla shifted uncomfortably in her seat. If he was on the same trail as she, bringing in outsiders would be a disaster. Hers was a personal quest.

"But I don't want to do it that way," Grizzly continued. "I won't deny I want to find the treasure myself."

"You want to sell it on the black market?" she asked, thinking of the way Grizzly had secretly claimed his family's inheritance.

"No. I don't know what I want to do, other than solve the mystery. And frankly, I'd rather work with you than with an outside party who will try to take over." He paused. "Assuming, of course, you have something to offer me beyond what I already know. And make no mistake, I'm aware of the legend that connects the Tuatha and the summit indicator atop Ben Macdui."

This was the moment of truth. Isla had to make a decision. Either she joined forces with Grizzly, or it would be a race to find the treasure with the American and whichever third party he brought in dogging her trail. With her limited resources, she really had no options. She reached into her purse, took out her journal, and opened it to the page she'd marked earlier.

"The Tuatha de Dannan still exist as an organization much like the so-called Illuminati in the States. Some believe they're on the wrong side of things. They've been blamed for terrorist attacks against those whom they deem outsiders, but I've seen nothing to indicate that. They're passionate about Celtic culture and tradition. They value their history."

Grizzly seemed unsurprised at this revelation. Apparently, this was another thing he already knew.

"In my research, I came across a letter, written in 1925 by a member of the Tuatha, alluding to a message embedded in the surface of the summit indicator, along with the code." She turned the journal around so he could see the string of letters and numbers she'd copied down. She gave him only a moment to look at it before she snapped it shut.

"All right," Grizzly said. "I propose we combine our efforts. You've got the code, which puts you one step ahead of me. I can offer my knowledge and experience. Also, I've got some money set aside to finance the search. Can you get away from your work?"

"I think so. My editor is apparently a fan of yours. If I tell her you're working on a new mystery and want to give us exclusive access, I'm sure she'll go for it."

"Excellent! We'll rest up here tonight and get started first thing in the morning." He narrowed his eyes and flashed a grin. "One room or two?"

Isla sighed. "The fact that you even have to ask doesn't speak well for your intuitive nature or your powers of deduction."

Grizzly laughed. "I get it. I just figure there's never any harm in asking. Won't happen again."

Isla rolled her eyes. What had she gotten herself into?

CHAPTER 9

National Museum of Scotland, Edinburgh

The National Museum of Scotland was comprised of two buildings set on a busy street in the heart of Edinburgh. Like the city itself, old met new in the architecture of the two main structures. The Museum of Scotland, which housed exhibits and artifacts relating to Scottish antiquities, culture, and history, featured modern architecture. By contrast, the Royal Museum, founded in the 1800s, boasted a more classical look, with a Victorian Romanesque Revival facade. This branch of the museum hosted collections covering science and technology, natural history, and world cultures. It was this half of the museum that Maddock and Bones planned to visit.

Inside, they passed through the Natural World section, featuring fauna from throughout history. Maddock took time to examine the T-Rex skeleton, while Bones paused to admire a triceratops skull.

"Let me guess," Maddock said. "You're trying to come up with a 'horny' joke."

Bones shook his head. "Nah, I was just thinking how awesome it would be to ride one of these things. Besides, a horny joke? That's low-hanging fruit. I expected better from you."

"When have you ever passed up low-hanging fruit?"

Bones held up a big hand. "Hold on. Are we talking chicks or humor?"

"Either one," Maddock said, examining a fully-reconstructed stegosaurus skeleton. "And before you tried riding a dinosaur, you might want to consider how you did on that mechanical bull in Austin."

"Screw you, Maddock. That had more to do with my level of sobriety than my riding abilities."

Maddock looked around and spotted a young man in a suit, one whom he recognized from photos on the web. As they drew closer, Maddock could read the man's museum ID badge, which named him Colin Jeong. This was the guy. They introduced themselves, and Jeong ushered them into his office.

"Colin Jeong," Bones said. "Those names don't usually go together."

"About as incongruous as a six-and-a-half foot tall Cherokee?" Jeong said, grinning. "My father is Korean, my mother Scottish. I inherited my dad's genes, but Mom passed along her love of Scotch whiskey."

"In that case, you and I are going to get along just fine," Bones said, squeezing into a small chair in front of Jeong's desk.

"I understand you've got a fossil you want identified and dated," Jeong said.

"Not exactly." Maddock had considered and discarded a dozen different ways to approach this conversation. He hoped Jeong would hear him out. "We have something we would like for you to identify, but it's not a fossil. As far as the date, we know it's from 1918."

Jeong frowned. "If that's the case, you don't need a paleontologist. Perhaps one of my colleagues in biological sciences would be better equipped to help you."

"Just show him, Maddock," Bones said.

Maddock reached inside his jacket pocket and removed a glass vial containing the tooth Bones had recovered from the wreckage of the U-boat. He handed it to Jeong.

The paleontologist's eyes went wide as he saw what he held in his hands. His jaw dropped, and he gaped as he slowly turned the vial, examining the tooth from every possible angle. And then he barked a laugh.

"Who put you up to this? Was it Joanna? I'll get back at her for this." His smile melted away as Bones stood, rising to his full height.

The big man leaned down, rested his hands on the desk, and locked eyes with Jeong.

"Listen to me, bro. This is no joke. That thing is real,

and we don't have time to mess around."

Jeong sat rigid. "But, it can't be." He held the tooth up between them. "Look at it. I'll admit, it's the most expertly done fake I've ever seen, but it's too fresh to be a prehistoric creature." He set the vial down on the desk. "Where did you get it?"

"We took it from the hull of a sunken German U-boat," Maddock said.

Jeong pushed back from his desk. "Gentlemen, I appreciate the laugh, but I'm busy. Please see yourselves out."

"You're starting to piss me off," Bones growled.

"Sit down, Bones," Maddock ordered, seeing the alarm in Jeong's eyes. "We're all friends here. Mister Jeong, I'm not going to waste time trying to convince you of anything. To speed things up, let's pretend you believe this item is genuine. If it were, what creature would you say it came from?"

Jeong's eyes flitted to his desk phone. He looked as though he was contemplating calling security to have the two treasure hunters kicked out of his office. But then he glanced at Bones, who sat glowering at him. He blanched.

Maddock could see the gears turning in Jeong's mind. How much damage could Bones do in the time it took security to get there, and would they be able to subdue him?

Jeong took a deep breath and nodded. "Fair enough. The sooner we get this over with, the sooner I can get back to work." He donned a pair of gloves, removed the tooth, and examined it at length with a magnifying glass. Finally, he replaced it in the vial and turned to his computer.

"Would you agree this is a match?" He turned his monitor around so Maddock and Bones could see a high-resolution image of a fossilized tooth.

"Looks like it to me," Bones said.

Jeong clicked through a series of images, all of which resembled the tooth they'd recovered.

"Now you see why I say it's impossible that this item is genuine. It appears to be from a plesiosaur."

From the corner of his eye, Maddock saw Bones smiling and nodding.

"What can you tell us about plesiosaurs?" Maddock asked. "Aside from their association with the Loch Ness legend." He already had some knowledge on the subject but hoped to set the scientist at ease with a softball question.

"The plesiosaur is a marine reptile from the Early Jurassic period. Long neck, thick body, powerful tail, four large flippers. They grew as large as fourteen meters long and four hundred fifty kilograms. Carnivorous. Needless to say, they are long extinct." Jeong kept his eyes locked on the tooth as he spoke, his voice trailing away. His resolve was clearly fading. "Would you permit me to study this tooth further? I could give you a definitive answer as to its authenticity, and perhaps learn more."

Maddock and Bones were more than happy to agree. It was, in fact, more than they had hoped for. After providing Jeong with their contact information, they excused themselves, hiding their triumphant smiles until they were well away from his office.

"We've got him," Bones said. "He's pretending he thinks it's a fake, but he knows the truth. I could see it in his eyes."

"I think you're right," Maddock said. "He's taken the bait. A little study and he'll be hooked."

As they once again passed through the dinosaur exhibit, Bones cast a longing glance at the triceratops skeleton.

"Remember what I was saying about how it would be awesome to ride one of those?"

"Yes?"

"They should make a sport out of it. You know, bring them back, Jurassic Park-style and then have a game where people ride them."

"Like polo?"

Bones pursed his lips, eyes narrowed, and tugged on his ponytail as he often did when thinking particularly hard. "Maybe, but more badass, hardcore."

Maddock's shoulders sagged. "Bones, that's the dumbest idea I've ever heard."

As they approached the exit, they passed a dark-haired man and an attractive woman with long, auburn hair. As usual, Bones managed to make eye contact with the woman and gave her a sly wink. She returned a tight-lipped smile and then they were gone.

"Not bad," Bones said.

"Did that guy she was with look familiar to you?" Maddock was sure he had seen the man before.

"She was with a guy? Sorry, I didn't notice."

"Of course you didn't."

Bones glanced back over his shoulder, searching the crowd. "She was really hot. I think I should go back and get her number."

"No time for that." Maddock opened the door and strode out into the bright, humid day. "We've got another stop to make."

CHAPTER 10

National Museum of Scotland, Edinburgh

"Tell me again who this guy is we're meeting?" Grizzly asked as they passed through the atrium.

"Walter Meikle. He's an old family friend." Despite the tenuous alliance they'd formed, Isla still resented answering the American's questions, especially the ones she'd already answered.

"And he's an archaeologist?"

"Archaeology is his profession, but he's also a historian and a skilled cryptologist. He's familiar with a variety of older codes. I'm hoping he'll be able to succeed where I've failed."

Using the writing on the summit indicator, she'd written down the Tuatha's coded message, but it had her stumped. It galled her to admit she couldn't decrypt it on her own. Then again, if it were a simple code, she'd worry that the treasure had already been found. The more challenging, the better, she supposed.

They found Meikle waiting for them in a small, cramped office. Shelves brimming with books lined every wall, leaving barely enough room for a desk and three cheap, metal and plastic chairs.

Meikle was a man of late middle age, with white hair, mustache, and beard. He had an easy smile and his eyes twinkled as he greeted them.

"I suppose we should get to business. What do you have for me?" he asked, once they'd exchanged pleasantries.

"A code." Isla handed him her notebook, opened to the page where she'd transcribed the letters from the summit indicator. "Needless to say, this remains between us. It's related to the family project."

"I understand completely." Meikle put on his reading glasses, but peered over the top of the lenses as he examined the book. "Interesting." After a few minutes of silent study, he looked up. "I assume you've tried the usual suspects?"

Isla nodded. "Simple substitution, Caesar Shift, all the common ones I could think of. No joy." Beside her, Grizzly nodded knowingly. She wondered if he actually had any idea what she was talking about.

Meikle stared at the page for a few more silent minutes. Suddenly, he dropped the notebook onto the desk, grabbed a legal pad and a pencil, and began scribbling furiously. Occasionally he paused, frowned, gave his beard a twist, and then got back to work.

Several minutes went by. Grizzly leaned in close to Isla and mouthed, "Do we need to be here for this?"

Isla had been wondering the same thing, but she didn't appreciate her new partner asking the question. She smirked and pointed to the door. She hoped her message was clear. *Go on and leave. No one's stopping you.* Unfortunately, he either didn't take her meaning or, more likely, didn't wish to leave without her.

Finally, Meikle breathed a soft, "Ah!"

Isla sat up a little straighter, hoping he'd made a breakthrough. Her heart sank as the man turned and began clicking away at his ancient keyboard.

At long last, he turned to face them, his face splitting into a wide grin.

"Did you crack it?" Grizzly asked.

"I have not yet *deciphered* the code," Meikle said with exaggerated patience. "But I can say with a fair amount of certainty that this is a Vigenère Cipher."

Grizzly was once again a bobblehead at the edge of her vision, but Isla pushed away her annoyance. "I've never heard of it."

"It's not very well known. In fact, it was once believed to be impossible to decipher. The secret is a five-letter keyword used as a starting point." He paused. "I don't suppose you have any idea what that word might be?"

Isla hesitated. She thought about the code, the Tuatha, and the treasure. A single five letter word sprang to the forefront of her mind. But to reveal it would mean revealing to Meikle the nature of her quest. She immediately realized her folly. He'd know what they were about as soon as he deciphered the code.

"Dagda," Grizzly said.

Isla flashed an angry look in his direction. It was one of the words she'd thought of. It's not that she wasn't going to tell Meikle; she simply wanted to be the one in charge. She sighed, knowing she was being childish.

"Either Dagda or Nuada," she said.

Meikle pursed his lips, stared at her for five uncomfortable seconds. Finally, he turned back to his computer. "Where did you get this code, Isla?" Forced nonchalance filled his voice.

"There's not a simple answer to that. It's the culmination of a lot of research and digging. You know…"

"…the family tradition." Meikle's shoulders sagged. "You're not just chasing legends this time. You're after the treasure of the Tuatha de Dannan, aren't you?" Before she could reply, he held up a hand. "I don't want to know. But I would discourage you from this path if I could."

"Why is that?" Grizzly asked.

"It's a fool's errand, and a dangerous one at that."

"If it's truly a fool's errand, then why is it so dangerous?" Grizzly persisted. "What's so deadly about the pot of gold at the end of the rainbow?"

"Because," Meikle said, turning in his chair to once again face them, "there are other fools who also believe in leprechauns."

"Fair enough," Grizzly said. "Did you decipher the code?"

"I did. Nuada was the keyword."

Isla felt a flash of triumph that Grizzly's offering had been incorrect. *Stop being a child,* she told herself. "What did you find?"

An odd expression passed over Meikle's face, as if he didn't want to tell them. He flashed a look of trepidation at Isla, but the damage was already done. Over his shoulder, she could see the answer on his computer screen. She provided the answer for him.

"Seek ye beneath Dun Monaidh."

Walter Meikle sat stock-still, smile firmly in place as Isla and her buffoon of a friend left his office. It was a shame, really. He'd known Isla's parents for a long time. In some ways, Meikle probably knew them better than she did. For that reason, he hated what he was about to do, but he had no choice.

"Should I have told her?" he whispered aloud. "Or would the knowledge put her in even greater danger?" He shook his head. He had no answer to either question, and it wasn't his place to make that decision. Not unless he wanted to potentially put his head on the chopping block.

He waited five heart-pounding minutes until he was certain the pair had gone. He couldn't have them returning unannounced and overhearing any part of the call he was about to make.

Hands trembling, he dug into the bottom of a desk drawer and took out an old address book. He flipped to the D's and found the entry for Dominic's Pizza. Both the name and the number had been struck through, but that was merely for show.

He took a deep breath, took out his phone, and punched in the number. It rang once and then someone picked up. No one spoke.

He cleared his throat and forced a hoarse "Hello?"

No answer. Was that someone breathing on the other end? He might as well try the code word.

"Tuatha," he said, with more conviction than he felt.

"Hold please." So there *was* someone at the other end.

Three rings and then someone picked up. More silence. Was common courtesy foreign to these people?

"This is Walter Meikle." Annoyance lent strength to his words.

"Well?" the voice said.

What was it with these dobbers? He'd been told, in no uncertain terms, to call this number if he should learn anything of value, and now they treated him as if he were an inconvenience.

"There has been a breakthrough in regard to certain items of historical value. I was told to call this number."

"Tell me," the speaker said in a clipped voice.

Meikle gave a brief sketch of the meeting that had just ended. He didn't mention Isla Mulheron by name, nor did he make mention of Smokey or whatever the American called himself. He kept it simple: the daughter of a former colleague had brought him information, a clue written in a cipher—a message which he'd managed to decrypt. He added a general description of the pair, enough that they could be recognized.

"And we can rely on this source?"

"Her father was reliable. This was a part of his papers." Meikle swallowed hard. That was not precisely what Isla had said. In fact, she hadn't said where she got the information, only that it related to her family's research. Why had he lied? Perhaps he should correct himself. No. That would only lead to more problems.

"Are you there?" the voice asked. "I said, I'm listening. What is this clue?"

Meikle relaxed. "Dun Monaidh."

CHAPTER 11

Maggie Dickson's Pub, Edinburgh

Drooping lavender flowers in window boxes and hanging baskets partially obscured the illuminated sign that marked Maggie Dickson's Whisky and Ale House, a tiny pub on Grassmarket Square. This busy, yet picturesque section of Edinburgh's Old Town featured pubs, shops, clubs, and hotels. Tourists mingled with locals going about their daily business. Here amidst buildings from the sixteenth century all the way up to recent vintage, Maddock felt the weight of history and truly appreciated how young his own country of origin was by comparison.

"You can check out the architecture later," Bones said, nudging Maddock with his elbow. "I need a drink." Leaving the sunny, crowded street, they headed inside.

The atmosphere inside the pub was exactly what Maddock expected—upbeat and noisy without being raucous. Chandeliers which hung from the painted ceiling shone down on dark wooden tables and darker wainscoting. Framed photos, neon signs, and football banners adorned the walls. Above the bar, a match played out on a widescreen television set.

"I'm not a soccer fan, but this works for me," Bones said. "Food smells good, too."

They paused to let a server pass by. The man carried two identical dishes—a coiled length of sausage atop mashed potatoes inside some sort of pastry.

"Never mind," Bones said. "That looks like a bowel movement. People really put that stuff in their mouths?"

Maddock laughed. "Suit yourself. I haven't eaten all day."

They made their way through the crowd and back to the area set aside for dining. Maddock immediately spotted a lanky, grey-haired man with thick glasses waving them over.

"You must be Maddock and Bonebrake. I'm Alban Calderwood." The man offered a liver-spotted hand to shake. Maddock took it and found Calderwood's grip was firm.

"Thank you for meeting us, Professor Calderwood," Maddock said.

"Any friend of Andrew Wainwright is a friend of mine. How is the old wankpuffin, anyway?"

Bones snorted a laugh. "I don't know what a wankpuffin is, but I'm stealing that one."

"It's a name I was never permitted to call my students. At least, not to their faces."

Maddock grinned. "We haven't visited Wainwright in a few years, but he sounded good on the phone." A retired professor and a descendant of the famed explorer Percy Fawcett, Wainwright had once helped Maddock and Bones in their search for a lost city in the Amazon.

"The telephone is the best way to experience Wainwright," Calderwood said. "That way, you don't have to look at his nose and ear hair, or risk being buried beneath a falling stack of books."

"I need to buy you a drink," Bones said. "What's good here? I saw a Guinness sign."

Calderwood's mouth twisted as if he'd just sucked a lemon. "Trust me; you want an Innis and Gunn. Best drink on tap here."

Bones bought a round for the table, and they settled in. Maddock found the ale quite to his liking. A hint of bitterness when it touched his tongue, but a fruity aftertaste with a touch of caramel.

"Nice," he said.

"It's really got an oaky afterbirth." Bones looked expectantly at his drinking companions, who exchanged puzzled looks. "It's a line from…oh, never mind." He took another swallow and looked around. "Tell me, who was Maggie Dickson? I saw a sign but didn't read it."

Calderwood winced. "You remind me of my students. 'Didn't read the chapter, Sir. I figured you were going discuss it anyway, so why bother?'"

"That's me," Bones agreed. "Except I'd have a chick read the chapter and give me the high points before class."

"Stop it." Laughing, Calderwood raised his hand to silence Bones. "You're bringing back unpleasant memories." He drained his glass and set the empty mug on the table. "Back to your question. Among other things, Grassmarket Square was a place where executions were held. Maggie Dickson was accused of drowning her own baby and was sentenced to hang. Her sentence was carried out in the Grassmarket. She was pronounced dead, but on her way to be buried, the wagon driver heard a knocking on the wooden coffin."

Maddock raised his eyebrows. "Oops."

Calderwood nodded. "They removed the lid to find Maggie very much alive. According to the law of the day, it was God's will that she live, so she was set free. The locals gave her the nickname Half Hangit' Maggie."

"Either someone botched the execution or she had quite a strong neck," Maddock said.

"Some believe she used her feminine wiles to manipulate the gaoler, who saw to it that the hangman engineered a weaker noose, but who can say for certain?"

"Leave it to Maddock to take a perfectly good story and analyze it to death," Bones said.

When their meals were ready, they dug in with gusto. Maddock enjoyed steak and ale pie, while Bones went with the Monster Burger—a tower of beef, cheese, bread, and onion rings. As they dined, Maddock finally revealed the reason he'd reached out to Calderwood. He filled the professor in on the sunken U-boat, the journal, and the artifacts they'd recovered.

"I know this is a longshot, but might you have any idea what this came from?" he asked, handing over the chunk of stone recovered from the strongbox.

Calderwood put on a pair of reading glasses and examined the black rock at length. While he continued his inspection, Maddock bought everyone another round. Lost in thought, Calderwood sipped at his ale.

Finally, he cleared his throat.

"You're certain your translation of the journal entry is correct?"

"Pretty sure," Bones said.

"It said 'they have been sitting on a false throne?' You're certain of that?"

"We are," Maddock said.

"In that case, there's only one thing it can be." Calderwood looked around, then lowered his voice. "The Stone of Destiny."

Bones sat up straighter. "Hold on. That's the stone that Scottish kings were crowned on, right?"

Calderwood nodded. "It is also known as the Stone of Scone. The English call it the Coronation Stone." He grimaced and took a swig of ale, as if to wash the words from his mouth.

"Time for the million dollar question," Bones said. "Do you think it's an alien artifact, the stone Jacob used for a pillow in the Bible story, or just a meteorite?"

Calderwood managed a tight smile. "Many far-fetched legends surround the stone—its origins, its composition, where it has been kept, whether or not it has powers. We could spend all day discussing them."

Bones smiled. "I'm down for that as long as the ale keeps flowing."

"So, this stone is lost?" Maddock asked.

Calderwood gave a noncommittal shrug. "Perhaps. Perhaps not."

"What does that mean?"

Calderwood's face grew stern, and he adopted a lecturing tone. "In 1296, Edward the First annexed Scotland and took the stone from Scone Abbey, where it was being kept at the time, and carried it back to Westminster Abbey. There it sat for centuries, to Scotland's shame. It was finally returned in 1996 and is now kept along with the crown jewels as Scotland's greatest treasures."

"So it's not lost," Maddock began, but Calderwood waved him into silence.

"Rumors persist that the stone that sits in the Crown Room is not the actual stone. Some say that the stone that came to Scone was not the genuine article; others say a false stone was substituted for it just ahead of the arrival of the English troops. What's more, the stone that is in the Crown's possession, the one that sat at Westminster Abbey and upon which English monarchs were crowned, is made of red sandstone, which has been definitively proved to be quarried near Scone. The problem is, the legends agree the stone was brought to Scone from elsewhere. And perhaps most important of all, though known only to a few scholars, the very oldest accounts describe the Stone of Destiny as being black and covered with markings." He held up the black chunk of rock for emphasis.

"That would explain the 'false throne' comment," Bones said. "The Kaiser would get a good laugh out of British royalty being crowned on a fake rock."

Maddock took a moment to digest this new information. "Let's assume a German spy did, in fact, break this stone off of the actual, authentic Stone of Destiny. Where should we begin looking?"

"Records show the stone was previously kept in an old fortress in Argyll and Bute in western Scotland. It's now the site of Dunstaffnage Castle. The legends I consider most reliable hold that the real stone never left there."

"Is Dunstaffnage near the water?" Maddock asked.

"Yes. In fact, what remains of it stands on a promontory near the coast, at Ardmucknish Bay, at the confluence of Loch Etive, Loch Linne, and the sea."

"It's not exactly close to where we found the sub, but if the Germans were hugging the coast, headed south..." Bones said.

"If you're on the trail of the true stone," Calderwood said, "Dunstaffnage is where I'd begin."

CHAPTER 12

Dunstaffnage Castle

Dunstaffnage Castle stood on a promontory overlooking Loch Etive to the north at the point where it met Loch Linne. Surrounded on three sides by water, the fourteenth-century fortress loomed dark and lonely in the seemingly perpetual mist. Isla and Grizzly strolled across the manicured lawn, the lush green carpet beneath their feet appearing unnaturally bright in contrast to the castle's dark gray walls.

As they approached, Isla took the time to admire the rugged beauty of the sturdy fortress. Unlike the ornate palaces of fairy tales, Dunstaffnage was built for a single purpose—defense. The quadrangular structure boasted rounded towers at three corners. In its heyday, it guarded the entrance to the Loch, and the Pass of Brander beyond.

"It's not as big as I imagined," Grizzly said. "The longest wall can't be much more than a hundred feet across, can it?"

"It's as large as it needed to be," Isla said, feeling defensive of one of her native country's landmarks.

"I wasn't criticizing," Grizzly said. "Just making an observation."

"Sorry. I'm on edge."

The truth was, Isla was embarrassed. Of the two of them, she'd considered herself the expert on the Tuatha treasure. Grizzly was a necessary annoyance, brought along so he wouldn't dog her trail with a film crew in tow. He'd surprised her the previous day when, after leaving Meikle's office, he'd suggested they head to Dunstaffnage. Isla's reminder that the clue had said "beneath Dun Monaidh," not "beneath Dunstaffnage," had led to a patronizing lecture about the history of the old castle.

This castle was built atop the ruins of Dun Monaidh,

a stronghold of the Gaelic kingdom of Dál Riata, supposedly founded by the legendary king Fergus the Great in the fifth century. Encompassing portions of present-day Ireland and Scotland, the Dál Riatan connection fit with the legend of the Tuatha and their Irish-Scottish link. Considering her family's background, Isla felt she should have already known that.

It wasn't that Grizzly knew something she didn't that bothered Isla. It was the superior attitude he'd adopted since that moment. He seemed to believe himself the leader and seized upon any opportunity to share useless information or to give orders.

"The Dunstaffnage Chapel is about five hundred feet that way," he said, pointing to the southwest. "There's not a whole lot left of it these days."

"You mean that ruined structure standing in plain sight? Thanks for pointing that out." She didn't try to temper her acerbic tone.

For his part, Grizzly seemed blissfully unaware of his effect on her. A permanent grin painted his face as they approached the castle.

"I do have to wonder," he said, "if this place hasn't been thoroughly excavated after all these years. If there was something beneath it, shouldn't it have been found by now?"

"We aren't necessarily expecting to locate the treasure here. We might only be looking for a clue. Something small or innocuous enough to have escaped notice."

Grizzly rubbed his chin and adopted a thoughtful expression ruined by his vacant stare. "Any ideas what that might be?"

Isla took out her phone and punched up a set of photographs. "As we discussed, the four symbols of the Tuatha are the spear, stone, sword, and cauldron." She swiped through, showing him images of each. "And then there's the goddess Danu. Any of these images might be an indicator of the presence of Tuatha, but wouldn't cause the average archaeologist or historian to bat an eye."

Grizzly nodded. "And since we're supposed to be looking 'beneath Dun Monaidh' I guess we should also look for trapdoors and hidden passageways."

Isla doubted archaeologists would have missed any secret doors, but she was growing tired of bickering with the man. She forced a smile, more like a grimace, and nodded. "Let's get on with it, then."

They spent the next two hours thoroughly inspecting the partially ruined fortress.

They examined every wall, poked around the foundations of the ruined east and west ranges, and scrutinized the corner towers. Nothing but big, gray blocks and lots of rubble. Grizzly had high hopes for the well, thinking it might afford passage to an area down below, but it had been filled in centuries ago. The gatehouse was a more recent addition and had been remodeled over the years, but they explored it too, paying particular attention to the basement. Still nothing. Hope fading, they climbed to the battlement level and followed the parapet walk around, looking down upon the grassy inner ward and the exterior from above.

"I think we need a new plan," Grizzly said.

Isla clenched her fists and clamped her jaws shut until she was certain she could reply without a trace of sarcasm. The breeze coming in off the water calmed her, and she breathed deeply. "What do you suggest?" she finally asked.

"Let's try the chapel." He pointed in the direction of the ruin. "There's not much left of it, but there's no harm in taking a look."

"It's worth a shot, I suppose." Isla doubted they'd find anything, considering how little remained of the house of worship, but no harm in looking.

As they walked, Grizzly launched into an impromptu and fully unnecessary lecture about the history of the Catholic Church in Europe, specifically its practice of absorbing pagan traditions as a means of linking its faith to that of the local populace and bringing new worshipers into the fold.

"The Bible actually forbids bringing a tree inside and decorating it, but that, along with gift-giving and other traditions, were absorbed into Christmas celebrations. Heck, Yuletide has connections to Odin, the wild hunt, and other pagan traditions. Christmas celebrations were actually low-key and kind of boring until the church started melding its practices with those of the pagan."

Isla squeezed her eyes closed and tried to tune him out. Of course, she immediately stumbled over a rock hidden beneath the lush grass. Grizzly caught her before she fell, which made matters worse.

"Try to watch where you're going," he said. "We'll probably cross rougher terrain than this before this is all over." Without missing a beat, he launched back into his lecture. "Did you know that Easter is linked to a pagan fertility goddess, which is why bunnies and eggs are part of the celebration? Birth, reproduction…"

"Grizzly," she said through gritted teeth, "I think we need to go back up to the parapet."

He stopped short. "Why is that?"

"So I can push you off."

Hurt flashed over his countenance, but only for a second, to be replaced by his trademark dimwitted grin. "I do talk a lot, don't I?"

"That's an understatement."

"Sorry," he said as they resumed their trek to the chapel. "When I do a cryptid video, I'm expected to keep talking pretty much the whole time. I never know what I might say that's actually worthwhile, so I say whatever comes to mind and we sort it out in editing."

Isla giggled, covering it immediately with a cough.

"Anyway," Grizzly continued, "all of my girlfriends complain about my lecturing. I guess it makes them feel embarrassed about all the things they don't know."

Isla felt her face turn scarlet. She thrust her hands into her pockets to keep from slapping him.

"Just try to keep it under control," she said.

"Will do."

The chapel proved to be a dead end. So little of it remained that, if there had ever been any Tuatha symbology included in the architecture, it was long gone. The ruins sat directly on the earth, what was once the floor now covered in a layer of gravel. Disheartened, Isla peered through one of the arched windows, back in the direction of the castle. What to do next?

As she gazed out, something caught her eye. But it couldn't be?

"What's wrong?" Grizzly asked.

"Those guys over there. I've seen them before." She pointed at two men, one tall with long, dark hair, the other a few inches shorter, with short blond hair. "They were entering the museum just as we were leaving."

"How can you be sure?"

"The big guy is a Native American. He's about six and a half feet tall, so he sticks out in a crowd. The blond man also stands out in his own way."

"Ah," Grizzly said. "Maybe they're just tourists?"

"Dunstaffnage is literally on the other side of the country from Edinburgh. That's an odd itinerary for someone who's sightseeing."

"You're right. I think we should shadow them and see what they're up to. If they're after the treasure, maybe they know something we don't."

Isla swallowed hard. She had no idea if the men were dangerous. They were both powerfully built and walked with an air of self-assurance, but she swore she'd seen a playfulness, almost impishness, in the bigger man's eyes when he'd looked her way.

"All right. Just keep your distance. I'll take the hot one."

"Which one would that be?" Annoyance rang in Grizzly's voice.

"The Indian is cute; the blond guy is hot."

"Fine," Grizzly sighed. "Just be careful."

CHAPTER 13

Dunstaffnage Castle

Bones couldn't help but feel a little bit disappointed in Dunstaffnage Castle. He'd expected something more expansive, and perhaps a bit more unattended. The castle was, however, impressive in its own way. He could imagine its stout walls standing up to attacks, its bulk casting an imposing shadow on enemy ships that tried to slip past. None the less, the old fortress looked as though any secrets it might have hidden had long ago been discovered.

"Not too promising, is it?" he asked.

"Too early to say," Maddock replied.

"It's just that this place kind of reminds me of Cliff Palace at Mesa Verde, if you know what I mean." That particular set of cliff dwellings had been taken apart and rebuilt by archaeologists, giving tourists an accurate depiction of what the site had once looked like, but destroying the feeling of authenticity that came with a mostly untouched ruin.

Maddock nodded. "I do. This is great for tourists, but it definitely has the feel of a place that's been thoroughly scoured before being opened to the public. Then again, you and I haven't explored it yet. Got your mojo working today?"

"Too early to tell. I'll see how much I can muster."

"Worst case, we wander around killing time until Jimmy comes up with something."

They moved through the old fortress, keeping an eye out for anything that might be a clue to the lost Stone of Destiny. They had just completed a circuit of the inner ward when a sudden movement caught Bones' eye. Someone had hastily moved around the corner of the gatehouse, much more quickly than someone merely strolling along. As he and Maddock continued on, he kept watch. Sure enough, a few seconds later, a face peered around the corner. He recognized her immediately.

"That's weird," he said.

Maddock quirked an eyebrow. "What is?"

"We're being followed."

As always, Maddock kept his cool. He didn't turn to look, or even break stride, trusting in Bones to tell him what he needed to know. "Description?"

"Remember that hot chick from the museum?"

"Can't say I do."

"Of course not." Bones flashed a rueful grin. "I know you're engaged to my sister, but you are allowed to look."

"Whatever. You're sure it's the same girl, and she's following us? I know you're charming, but to drive all the way across the country just to stalk you? That's a bit much."

"Laugh it up, bro. It's her, and I'm one hundred percent certain she's watching us. What's more, she's trying and failing to keep from being seen."

Maddock ran a hand through his close-cropped hair, jaw set, eyes narrowed in concentration. "Let's split up. She'll follow one of us…"

"Me, of course," Bones said, enjoying the affronted look on Maddock's face.

"It's possible she could have a thing for me."

"Yeah, and it's also possible that frozen crap from an airplane toilet could land on your head, but the odds are pretty freaking slim. I will, however, keep my hopes up."

"About the toilet or the girl?"

Bones pointed up at the sky.

Maddock smirked. "Anyway, as I was saying, how about we split up? She follows one of us, the other follows her, try to get an idea of what she's up to before we confront her."

"Let me do the confronting. If she's into me, I don't want to blow my chances."

Shaking his head, Maddock turned and wandered over to check out the well, while Bones made a show of casting a baleful look around at the castle. He gave a shake of his head and then headed out to inspect the exterior walls. He tried to act naturally, but the sensation of having a target painted on his back was like an itch he couldn't scratch.

He moved along the wall in the direction of the steep embankment that ran down to the water. He came to a corner tower and, as he rounded, glanced back. Sure enough, the woman was following him. He reached the next tower and glanced back again. Still trailing along behind him. He decided to have a bit of fun. Once he was out of sight, he took off at a run, rounding the next corner at a breakneck pace.

It wasn't long until he'd almost made a complete circuit of the old fortress, and he spotted something odd. A sturdily-built man with wavy brown hair was creeping along in a series of comical attempts at concealment. As Bones watched, the fellow dashed twenty paces to a stray boulder, flattened himself on the grass, then rose up to peer over it. A few seconds later he repeated the maneuver. He never actually looked back, so Bones was able to tag along behind him. The fellow reached the corner tower. When he peered around, Bones got a good look at his face.

"He was with the hot chick," Bones whispered. "What's he doing?"

He had his answer a moment later when he saw the fellow hit the dirt as, in the distance, a blond man glanced back his way.

"Holy freaking crap." Bones had to roll his eyes. "I'm following this dude. He's following Maddock, who's following the hot chick. Which means she's somewhere behind me." He turned on his heel and strode back in the direction of the greenspace that separated the castle from the parking area. It was time to find out just what the hell was going on here. He was considering his approach when he heard a shrill scream.

"That can't be her."

He took off at a sprint and burst out onto the green lawn seconds later. At the edge of his peripheral vision, he spied Maddock running toward him. Maddock pointed in the direction of the parking lot. Bones turned and immediately saw what his friend had spotted.

The attractive young woman who'd been spying on him minutes before was being dragged away by a man in a suit.

Bones swore as he poured on the speed, his long legs eating up the distance between them. He had no idea what sort of danger he might be running toward. What was more, he was doing it on behalf of a complete stranger—one who had just been stalking him.

"This," he muttered, "is un-be-freaking-lievable."

CHAPTER 14

Dunstaffnage Castle

Isla struggled to shout for help but the man had one arm locked around her throat in a powerful chokehold, and her cry of desperation came out as a gurgled whimper. She dug in her heels, tearing furrows in the soft turf. He was impossibly strong and had no difficulty hauling her along. She fought and clawed, trying to break free. He let out a curse as her fingernails dug into the back of his hand.

A series of images flickered, strobelike, across her vision as she thrashed: her captor's fair skin and brown hair, the gray sky, the green grass, the ruined castle, a man running. With the images came a flood of questions. Who was her captor? Why was he taking her? Was she going to die? How had she let this happen? She'd been so focused on watching the Indian that she hadn't heard this man creeping up on her. What if he was working with the Indian and his partner?

"Hurry up!" a voice shouted.

"You want to help me?" her captor replied. "I think she's had a few too many scones. She's a heavy one."

Irrationally, Isla wanted to inform the man that she worked out regularly, but her more immediate concern was the fact he was dragging her toward a silver SUV that sat idling in the car park. What could she do?

And then, the man released her. She fell hard to the ground, her breath leaving her in a rush.

She looked up to see the Indian kneeling over her. His partner, the blond man, flashed past them and slammed into her fleeing abductor. They crashed to the ground, the blond man rolling and coming up to his feet in a fighting stance.

"It's okay. I've got you," the Indian said.

Isla scooted backward on her bottom, but the big man seized her by the upper arms and picked her up as if she were weightless. She knew in an instant that, compared to the man who had initially seized her, this was the far more dangerous of the two.

"Calm down," he said, releasing her and holding out his big hands, fingers splayed. "We don't mean you any harm."

"Let her go!" Grizzly came running toward them. He skidded to a halt, ten paces away, and stood, fists clenched, elbows cocked. Had the situation not been so dire, Isla would have laughed at the absurdity of his posturing in the face of the much larger man. He looked like a bantam rooster facing down an eagle.

"Bro, you need to chill. I've got to help my friend," the big man said.

In response, Grizzly picked up a small stone and flung it at him. It went wide, cracking the windscreen of a nearby jeep.

"Dude, don't piss me off. Just keep an eye on her." With that, the man turned and ran toward his friend, who was now chasing the man who'd tried to seize Isla.

"Let's get out of here." Grizzly took her by the wrist and tried to lead her to their car, but something kept her locked in place.

The roar of an engine and the squeal of tires cut across the sounds of pursuit as her kidnapper's accomplice—the man who'd been waiting in the idling SUV—peeled out. The vehicle shot across the car park, headed in the direction of the driver's fleeing accomplice. As they watched, he stuck his arm out of the window.

"He has a gun." Isla gasped. "Look out!"

A series of loud, sharp bangs rolled across the car park.

The running men scattered. Moments later, the SUV skidded to a halt long enough for the failed kidnapper to jump in, and then they were away.

"What just happened?" Grizzly asked. "Who the hell were those guys?"

Isla slowly shook her head. "Which ones? The

kidnappers or the guys who saved me?"

Grizzly threw up his hands. "None of this makes sense. The men who saved you are the same ones who were stalking us?" He took a deep breath. "They're headed back this way. Let's just get the hell out of here."

"No." Isla wasn't completely sure why, but she sensed she could trust these men. Furthermore, she wanted answers.

"Isla, are you crazy? Just because they saved you doesn't mean they aren't dangerous. Maybe we're dealing with two sets of kidnappers, and one pair chased the other away, and now they're coming back for us."

"Or maybe they're only following the same trail as us, in which case we have a common enemy."

Grizzly let out a scornful laugh. "I've worked in television long enough to know that the enemy of your enemy is not always your friend."

"This isn't television," she said, watching as her two rescuers strode purposefully toward them.

"We're searching for a lost treasure, you almost got kidnapped, but you got saved by a giant Indian. Sounds like Hollywood to me."

"You can run if you want to," she said. "I'm going to find out who they are and what they want."

"Fine." He scanned the ground until he found another rock.

"Don't do it," Isla said. "You'll just make them mad."

"Whatever you say." He slipped the stone into his pocket and stood, hands on hips, waiting for the men.

The two men stopped ten paces away, and they regarded one another for a few silent seconds before the blond man finally spoke.

"So, are you two good guys or bad guys?"

CHAPTER 15

Dunstaffnage Castle

Maddock couldn't help but notice how beautiful the woman standing before him was. Long, wavy auburn hair framed a creamy complexion. Her intense, hazel-eyed gaze caused his breath to catch in his throat. Realizing he was staring, he gave his head a quick shake. What was he thinking?

The woman didn't seem to notice. "Thank you for the rescue. I'm Isla Mulheron, and you are…"

"Dane Maddock." They shook hands. She had soft hands but a solid grip. "This is my partner, Bones Bonebrake."

For once, Bones wasn't checking out the attractive woman in their midst. He stood, frowning down at Isla's companion, a stocky, brown-haired man.

"You look really familiar," Bones said. "Where do I know you from?" And then his eyes brightened. "You're Grizzly Grant! The cryptid hunter."

Grizzly smiled and gave a single nod, like a monarch accepting tribute. "You would be correct. Always a pleasure to meet a fan."

Bones turned to Maddock. "This dude is a legend in cryptozoology circles, especially on the forums. He's investigated some jacked-up stuff."

Maddock shook hands with Grizzly. As he did so, he could have sworn he saw Isla roll her eyes.

"Any idea who those guys were who tried to grab you?" Maddock asked.

"No idea," Grizzly said.

At the same time, Isla said, "The Tuatha."

"Wait. The Tuatha de Dannan?" Bones said sharply.

Isla nodded. "So, you are after the treasure?"

Bones and Maddock exchanged glances.

"Sort of," Bones said.

"We're after *a* treasure," Maddock added. "Are the

two of you looking for the Stone of Destiny?" Maddock asked. "That's what we're focused on at the moment."

Isla frowned. "The Stone of Destiny? But it's not missing."

Grizzly held up a finger. "Not so fast. That all depends on who you ask."

A tangled conversation broke out between Bones, Isla, and Grizzly. Each person did a great deal of talking and very little listening. Maddock pressed his hands to his temples, took a deep breath, and raised his voice.

"All right! Everybody take a breath."

They cut off their conversation abruptly, and silence reigned as they gazed at him. Bones grinned, Isla appeared confused, while Grizzly looked downright affronted.

"I don't know whether or not we're all on the same trail, but we've run afoul of the same people I think we should compare notes, but not here. We don't know if those guys will come back, and I don't know about the two of you, but Bones and I aren't armed."

Tires screeched as the SUV careened along the narrow country road. The lush, green landscape flashed past his window, but Brown barely saw it. They had failed badly.

They crested a hill and Campbell hit the brakes as a stray cow wandered across their path.

Brown's head snapped forward, and he instinctively grabbed the dash with both hands.

"Hells bells, Campbell. You're going to kill us if you don't have a care. We're well away from them."

"And I want to keep it that way," Campbell snapped. "We don't need them catching up with us. You already got yourself seen."

"If you'd helped me, like I said, instead of waiting in the car, we'd already be away with the girl."

"Bollocks." Campbell rolled down the driver's window and spat a wad of phlegm on the speed limit sign as they zoomed by. "Did you see how fast those blokes were? Especially that big fellow with the long hair.

What was he, anyway?"

"American Indian from the looks of him," Brown said. "But he wasn't supposed to be with them."

When they'd been sent to Dunstaffnage with instructions to search for any clues relating to the ancient Tuatha de Danann, they'd also been provided with a description of a man and woman whom they might encounter. The pair supposedly had information the Tuatha needed. Their orders had been to shadow them and find out what the pair knew. He and Campbell had done so at first, but it soon became apparent that they would learn nothing by following the two around.

Brown let out a long sigh. The attempted abduction had been his decision. When he'd finally gotten close enough to recognize the woman, he'd panicked. Now he was wondering what to do next.

"You know we've got to go back," he said.

Campbell looked at him as if he were crazy. "The situation has changed. There are four of them; not the two we were initially told about. And at least two know how to handle themselves. If Fairly wants us to explore Dunstaffnage, he can bloody well give us a few more men. Besides, that girl and her friend obviously didn't know anything. They were wandering around like lost sheep."

"You didn't recognize the girl, did you?"

Campbell shook his head. "Should I have done?"

"It was Isla Mulheron."

This time Brown didn't catch himself when Campbell slammed on the brakes. His neck and spine wrenched from the force of their stop as they skidded to a halt in the middle of the road.

"Tell me you're joking." Campbell's face was ghostly pale in the midday light. "You

Brown shook his head.

"But she's hands-off. Watch and report. Always has been."

"I know." Brown buried his face in his hands. "I saw her, and something said the fastest way to find out what she knew was to grab her and…"

Campbell squeezed the steering wheel in a white-knuckled grip. "You panicked."

"I know. We can't let Fairly know we failed, and we certainly can't tell him we tried to grab Mulheron."

"You tried to grab her," Campbell corrected.

Brown nodded, still not quite able to believe how badly he'd botched this assignment.

"The only way out of this is to finish the job," Campbell said. "We'll go back tonight and find whatever it is we're supposed to find. That or make damn well sure there's nothing there."

"And what if her men give us trouble again?"

Campbell shrugged. "Kill them."

Isla and Grizzly led them to a pub a short drive from the ruins of Dunstaffnage. Trying to blend in with the locals, not an easy task with Bones in their party, they settled around a small table, ordered pints of an ale called Skull Splitter, and compared notes on their respective searches.

Maddock recounted the discovery of the U-boat, the tooth, the captain's journal, and showed them the strange black rock. Isla examined the stone with interest. She had some familiarity with the legend of the Stone of Destiny but was interested in Calderwood's take on it. She quickly impressed Maddock with her keen mind and insightful questions. Several times he had to remind himself that he was in a committed relationship. At least, he thought he was.

Disappointed that they had not brought the tooth with them, Grizzly gave the stone a cursory inspection and immediately launched into speculation about its alien origins. Bones grinned and nodded along, visibly hanging on the man's every word.

Isla's story took a bit longer, as she brought Maddock up to speed on the history of the Tuatha de Dannan. Bones and Grizzly had apparently heard it all before and busied themselves swapping legends of lake monsters. By the second round of drinks, Grizzly was regaling his one-man audience with an improbable story of a Finnish lake monster and lost Nazi troops, though he couldn't seem to make up his mind whether it was a squad, platoon, or regiment.

In contrast to the cryptid hunter, whom Maddock thought was a windbag, Isla was bright, witty, and articulate. They shared a mutual interest in history, and she'd also done some climbing, which was one of Maddock's passions. Several times he caught himself steering the conversation away from the topic at hand and in a more personal, get-to-know-you direction. Each time he found himself, he quickly returned to the subject of treasure hunting.

She told him about the treasure of the Tuatha: the spear, the sword, the stone, and the cauldron.

"You honestly believe in it?" Maddock asked.

"Searching for the treasure of the Tuatha is sort of a family tradition. My parents," she hesitated, "believed in it too."

Maddock didn't miss her use of the past tense, but he chose not to press her on it.

"I know it sounds far-fetched," she went on, "but I guess I'm a true believer. Not much better than those two." Her eyes darted to Bones and Grizzly, who were laughing about a viral video of an alleged river monster that both agreed was nothing more than a fishing net caught on a log.

"Sure it wiggled back and forth," Bones was saying.

"Because of the current," Grizzly finished.

"Don't be so hard on yourself," Maddock said. "Bones and I have been doing this for a long time, and we've found some things that no one would have believed were real."

"Really?" She leaned in close enough that Maddock caught the scent of her perfume. It reminded him of vanilla, coffee, with a faint hint of something woodsy. "And what sorts of things would those be?"

Her smile sent a hot flash from the base of his neck

down to his spine, and he shifted uncomfortably in his seat. This part was always awkward. Upon meeting someone new, if he or Bones revealed too much too soon, they'd be thought a couple of crackpots. If they came across as hiding something, however, it could impede the building of trust.

"We found the Amber Room, for one," he whispered.

Isla sat up ramrod straight. "You're lying," she accused. "Word would have gotten out."

Maddock shook his head. "We were in the SEALs. Top-secret mission. Everything classified."

She gaped at him, then barked a laugh. "You're winding me up."

"Look me in the eye," he said, leaning closer. "I swear it's true."

That was a mistake. Isla gazed into his eyes much longer than Maddock thought necessary. Her face seemed to swim toward his, her eyes drew him in, and he had the strange sensation of falling forward. Damn, she was beautiful.

"All right. I believe you." Her words broke the spell. They both sat back and took long pulls of ale. He thought he noticed a pink hue to her cheeks as she drank.

"Where is it?" she whispered.

"Can't tell you. Like I said; classified government stuff."

She stuck out her lower lip in a delicate pout. "Be that way, then. What else have the two of you found?"

"More than our share of treasure," he said. "Lots of other stuff, some of it pretty crazy, but we'll have to get to know one another better before I elaborate."

"*Are* we going to get to know each other better, Mr. Maddock?" Her eyes flitted to his left hand, and then back to his face.

"I hope so." He cleared his throat. "About this treasure. I think I see a connection between our two searches."

"The stone that cries out beneath the king when he claims his throne," she said.

"Exactly. It sounds very much like a stone that monarchs would sit upon when crowned, doesn't it?"

"But where do we look?" Bones asked. Apparently, he and Grizzly had wrapped up their water monster conversation and had started paying attention to their companions. "Both our trails led to Dunstaffnage, but it doesn't seem like anything's there."

"There has to be," Isla said. "It's too great a coincidence that, despite following different clues, we both ended up there, along with whoever is chasing us."

"The modern descendants of the Tuatha," Maddock said.

"Probably," Isla said.

"Back to the treasure," Grizzly interjected. "We went all over that place with a fine-tooth comb, and I don't think there's any treasure or even any clues there. At least, not anymore."

"Unless it's buried deep," Isla added.

Maddock's phone vibrated. He was pleased to see it was a lengthy message from Jimmy. Along with the other projects he'd given his old friend, he'd asked him to research Dunstaffnage. As usual, Jimmy did not disappoint. He grinned as he read the message.

"Actually, it looks like Dunstaffnage might still have some secrets to give up." He looked around the table, smiled. "Does anyone here feel like going for a dive?"

CHAPTER 16

Dunstaffnage Castle

"This looks like the correct spot." Maddock looked up at the hulking silhouette of Dunstaffnage, inky black against the moonless sky. His eyes ran down the edge of the eastern tower, then followed along to the distinctive stone outcropping that hung just above where they stood. When he was sure they were in proper alignment, he turned to face the water, took out his compass, and got his bearings.

"According to this Jimmy guy, there's a passageway down beneath the water, but it's a dead end?" Grizzly asked.

"Yes," Maddock said through gritted teeth. He wasn't happy with the decision that Grizzly should accompany him on this dive, but the man had pushed hard, arguing that one representative from each party should be included. Maddock didn't appreciate the insinuation that he and Bones would double-cross their new partners, but he understood the lack of trust, as they'd only met earlier that day. Furthermore, the cryptid hunter had used his connections to borrow the SCUBA gear they needed on short notice. That earned him a few points on Maddock's scorecard.

Maddock had expected Bones to object to being left behind. After all, the big Indian loved to dive. Unfortunately, he'd gotten no help from that quarter. Bones seemed to have finally taken notice of Isla, and was now eager to "keep an eye on her" in case the men who'd tried to abduct her returned. Maddock wasn't sure how he felt about leaving the two of them alone, but he chose not to dwell on that thought.

"Well, if there's any kind of hidden door, I'll be sure to find it," Grizzly said. "Did I tell you about the trapdoor I discovered in that haunted house in Connecticut?"

"I thought it was a cover over the old septic tank," Maddock said, focusing on the illuminated face of his dive compass.

"It was, but it was totally hidden. No one knew it was there before I found it."

"Before you fell in?" Maddock asked absently.

"I didn't fall. I climbed down in. And then I slipped." Grizzly lapsed into silence. Apparently, the memory was not a pleasant one.

"Okay, here's what we're going to do. I've got our bearings. The way in should be about a hundred meters that way." He pointed in the direction the compass indicated.

"You don't have to go metric," Grizzly said. "We're both American."

Maddock silenced him with a blank stare. "Like I said, I've got the bearing. Stay on my six and wait for me to signal you when I've found the passageway. I'm more broadly built than you, so I'll go first. According to the accounts Jimmy found, it's pretty rocky and uneven through there, and it could be easy to get stuck. If I get a fin tangled or something, I might need your help to get free. Got it?"

"Don't worry. You're safe with me." Grizzly clapped a hand on Maddock's shoulder. "I know diving at night can be scary, but I've done it plenty of times. You'll be fine."

Maddock sighed. "Just try not to get lost."

They waded out into the cool waters of Ardmucknish Bay until they were deep enough to begin swimming. Visibility was almost nil and the current steady in his face as Maddock propelled himself through the water with powerful kicks. The beam of his headlamp sliced through the murky water, illuminating the rocky seabed below. A flicker of light told him Grizzly was keeping pace. That was good. Maddock would feel obligated to go back for the man should he lose his way. At least the cryptid hunter wasn't slowing him down.

He kept an eye on his compass, mentally tracking the

distance they'd covered. When he estimated they'd gone a hundred meters, he came to a halt. He was utterly unsurprised when, a few seconds later, Grizzly collided with him. He shoved the man away, held up his hands to indicate, *You stay here*, and then he dove.

He had a feeling Dunstaffnage would not be giving up its secrets easily. The jumble of rocks beneath the surface of the water seemed to go on forever, and one stone looked much the same as the next. This was not a problem. He was a patient man, even meticulous when the situation called for it. He could work a grid with the best of them, usually to the chagrin of Bones and the rest of the crew. Laughing internally at the thought of Grizzly treading water against the current while Maddock slowly explored underwater, he selected a starting point and began the search.

He swam back and forth, gradually working outward from his selected point. Light flashed across his field of vision. Apparently Grizzly was trying to help by adding his beam to that of Maddock's headlamp. Maddock waved him away.

Finally, something caught his eye—a spot that was completely free of sand, silt, or debris. In its midst lay a deep shadow that proved to be a man-sized hole. Maddock felt the current pushing back against him. It would be a challenging swim, but the trip back out should be easy if they didn't tarry too long. He turned, got Grizzly's attention, and gave him a thumbs-up. Grizzly returned the signal and dove. Moments later, he shouldered past Maddock and swam into the narrow channel. Maddock bit down on his regulator, imagining he was a Kraken biting Grizzly's head off and followed along.

They hadn't gone far before Grizzly began to tire. Twice he stopped, bracing himself against the sides of the passage in order to keep the current from pushing him back. Maddock wondered if a well-placed jab from his Recon knife would get the man going again. Finally, Grizzly moved on, and after a short swim, the channel opened up, ending at a blank wall.

Maddock swam to the surface and clambered out onto a narrow ledge. Grizzly surfaced a few seconds later, spat out his regulator, and clutched the ledge. Maddock pretended to busy himself with his gear while Grizzly sucked in ragged breaths and struggled to climb out of the water. After about twenty seconds, Maddock could no longer deal with his own pettiness and reluctantly hauled his unwelcome partner up onto dry land.

"Thanks," Grizzly gasped. "I wore myself out breaking the current for you."

"Breaking the current?"

"I went first so I could block the current. That way it was easier for you—like one race car drafting behind another."

"Sure," Maddock said.

They removed their air tanks and moved along the ledge, searching the darkness with their headlamps, until they came to a dead end.

"This doesn't look like what your friend described," Grizzly said. "Think we took the wrong passageway?"

Maddock shook his head. "The odds of there being more than one channel like this are microscopic."

"I don't know. You ever hear of Oak Island? That place is riddled with underwater passages."

Maddock bit back a retort. Would this guy never shut up?

"It looks like the ceiling caved in. Let's see if we can move some of this rubble."

They set to work, Grizzly laboring without complaint until they'd cleared a large enough opening to squeeze through. On the other side, Maddock found what they were looking for.

Jimmy had discovered an archived post from a defunct internet forum, written by a man who claimed that, while diving, he'd found the underwater passageway, which took him beneath Dunstaffnage Castle. There, he'd found a wall covered in odd, ancient-looking carvings. Sure enough, here was that same wall.

"This is really something," Grizzly said. He played his light back and forth across the solid wall. "It looks legit to me."

Maddock nodded. This was nothing like the fake pictographs vandals sometimes carved among genuine, historical images. These were very old, weathered by perhaps centuries of water dripping down from above. He saw no apparent pattern to the carvings, which were a mixture of stars, letters, numbers, and symbols. He took out his waterproof camera and snapped a series of pictures.

"Do you think this is a clue to the location of the stone?" Grizzly asked.

"No telling," Maddock said. "Maybe there's a code here that needs to be deciphered, although I have to admit it seems unlikely. The images are too irregular."

"There has got to be something here," Grizzly said. "This place is almost impossible to get to, so it's not like rock carvings in the American southwest, where people would camp for the night beneath an outcropping and leave a little graffiti behind. Somebody carved this here for a reason."

Maddock couldn't disagree. He took a few steps back and examined the symbols one by one. He was about halfway done when Grizzly let out a triumphant cry.

"That one! I recognize it." He pointed to a shape like an old grave marker in the lower portion of the carving. "This is one of the symbols that represent the Tuatha de Dannan treasure."

They both moved closer to inspect it.

"Are you sure it's Tuatha?" Maddock asked.

"Definitely. I've been studying up on the treasure forever. Isla and I also spent a lot of time going over them. There's the spear, the sword, the cauldron, and this one is the stone."

"Well, the stone *is* what we're looking for," Maddock said.

Frowning, Grizzly rose up on his tiptoes and shone

his light down into the recessed area where the stone symbol was carved. "This is weird. The edges around the image are cut deep. It's almost like a handle." Without warning, he hooked two fingers into the carving and pulled.

"Grizzly, no!" Maddock grabbed the man's wrist and yanked his hand away, but it was too late. The oblong shape that represented the Tuatha stone tilted forward, then snapped back into place when Grizzly's hand came free.

The floor trembled beneath their feet, and a low rumbling filled the cavern. Instinctively Maddock looked up, fearing the ceiling might collapse. But the sound stopped.

"See?" Grizzly said. "Nothing to worry…"

His words were lost among a series of sharp cracks as the floor fell away beneath their feet and they tumbled into darkness.

CHAPTER 17

Dunstaffnage Castle

Bones lay back on the soft grass, fingers laced together behind his head, and gazed up at the starry night. After hours, the ruins of Dunstaffnage were about as quiet as a place could get. A perfect locale for some alone time with a lovely lady. The problem was, Isla didn't seem to feel the same way. The auburn-haired beauty had shown no interest in him. She now sat a few feet away, knees pulled against her chest, staring balefully out at the water.

"How long do you think it's going to take them?" she asked.

"There's no way of telling. Depends on how long it takes to find the underwater passageway, and then what's waiting for them at the other end. Maddock won't waste time, though. He's efficient."

"I just hope they're all right."

"Don't worry about them. Maddock's the most capable man I know, except for me, of course." He smiled and winked, but she was still gazing off into the distance, paying him no mind.

"It's not Maddock who concerns me. I'm worried that Grizzly will do something stupid and get them both into trouble." A breeze gusted in from across the water, and she shivered.

"If you're cold, you can come sit next to me," Bones said, trying to sound both innocent and inviting at the same time. The flinty stare Isla shot in his direction caused him to immediately abandon any thoughts of making a connection with her, at least not tonight. He changed tactics on the fly. "Grizzly seems okay to me."

Isla rolled her eyes. "The man is a buffoon. He has just enough knowledge to get himself into trouble."

"But he's a well-known cryptid hunter. He's spent plenty of time in the field, built a reputation for himself, stayed alive in some precarious situations."

"The fact that he hasn't gotten himself killed tells me he's got more dumb luck than Forrest Gump. That or he's done a deal with the devil."

Bones couldn't believe what he was hearing. "Sounds like you've got a personal grudge against him. Maybe he's not paying you what you're worth?"

Isla let out a harsh laugh. "I don't work for that idiot. Circumstances brought us together, and I thought he would do less damage if I kept an eye on him."

"Circumstances? Like a romance gone bad?"

"Oh my God." Isla sprang to her feet and began pacing.

Bones watched her stalk back and forth, reading the lines of her face, the set of her jaw until he sensed it was safe to speak again. "Sorry. Didn't mean to get under your skin."

"It's fine. You'll understand after you've worked with him for a few days. It might not even take that long for you to figure him out."

Bones was dying to ask more questions, to understand what, exactly, had caused the rift between Isla and Grizzly. He and the cryptid hunter had talked lake monsters and sea monsters for a good half-hour and the guy knew his stuff. There had to be something else going on here.

"Look, if there's a problem with Grizzly, Maddock and I should know about it if we're going to work together."

"I told you what the problem is; he's a tosser. I don't…" She jerked her head around, looking in the direction of the parking lot. "Do you hear that?"

Bones was already on his feet. He'd caught the sound of tires crunching gravel and asphalt. In the dim light, his sharp eyes spotted the outline of an SUV, headlights turned off, rolling into the parking lot. They, whoever they were, had even cut the engine and were coasting in.

"Someone isn't taking any chances," he said. "I'm pretty sure it's the same guys from earlier today."

"Good thing we parked down the road," Isla said.

"We can take them by surprise."

"*We* aren't doing anything. They tried to snatch you earlier, and they might try it again, so you keep out of sight."

"Fine. I will."

Bones heard the lie in her voice but didn't waste time arguing.

From the corner of the castle, they watched as two men emerged from the car. After a few seconds, they flicked on a pair of flashlights and separated. One headed in the ruined chapel while the other made a beeline for the castle.

"What are we, I mean you, going to do?" Isla whispered.

"Look, chick. I've been doing this for a long time, so I'm asking nicely. Please stay the hell out of sight and let me handle it?"

Isla let out a huff of breath, turned, and vanished into the darkness.

Bones relaxed. One less thing to worry about. He watched as the flashlight beam bounced its way toward the castle. The man moved along at a jaunty pace, clearly thinking he and his friend had the place to themselves. That was all right with Bones.

He watched as the man moved to the castle entrance and began working at the lock that held the gate in place. Perfect! His quarry distracted by the task at hand, Bones melted into the night and circled around behind him. Growing up, he'd learned from his grandfather how to move silently in the forest, so treading soundlessly on the soft grass outside the castle was child's play. In a matter of seconds, Bones was standing behind the man.

"Don't move," he said.

The man didn't follow directions very well. He spun about, one hand reaching inside his jacket.

Bones struck him flush on the jaw. It was a solid blow that turned the man's knees to rubber. Bones hit him again for good measure, pinned him to the ground, and relieved him of the small automatic pistol he had tucked in a belly band beneath his shirttail. Hastily, he tied his captive up with his own shoelaces and then took his wallet.

Bones recognized the man immediately as the driver of the car; the one who had taken potshots at him and Maddock. He checked the man's license. "Theodore Campbell," he read aloud. "You go by Ted? Teddy? Mister T?"

The man narrowed his eyes and glared up at Bones. "Bugger off."

Bones slapped him hard across the ear. "This will end a lot better for you if you mind your manners," he said. "You get what I'm saying, Teddy?"

"The name is Campbell."

"Whatever. Tell me, *Campbell.* Who do you work for?"

Hatred burned in Campbell's eyes. "I already gave you the only answer you're going to get."

"Yeah, but it was the wrong answer." Bones knew time was tight. The man's partner might show up at any moment. His patience waning, he shoved his hand into Campbell's mouth, grabbed one of his incisors, and twisted.

Campbell let out a yelp, which Bones quickly muffled with his hand.

"I flunked out of dental school, so it only gets worse from here. You ready to talk now?"

Eyes wide, Campbell nodded.

"All right. Who do you work for?"

"I'm one of the Tuatha de Dannan. I don't work for them; I'm one of them."

"And what are you doing here?"

"You are trying to take what rightfully belongs to us." He hesitated but hurried on when Bones made to grab another tooth. "The treasure."

"How did you know we would be here looking for it?"

"We have our ways." A grin split his face, maniacal laughter in his eyes. "You might be thinking of killing me, but it would be a waste of time. Even if you end me and my partner, more will follow."

Bones interrogated the man for another minute, but the fellow knew nothing, aside from the orders he'd been given—come to Dunstaffnage, search for clues to the treasure of the Tuatha. If he met Isla, he was to find out what she might know. Bones also extracted the name of the man's partner—Brown. Satisfied, he gagged Teddy and left Isla to watch over him. She refused to take the gun but accepted Bones' Recon knife instead. From the look in her eyes, Bones had a feeling she was hoping Teddy would give her a reason to use it.

He crept down to the ruined chapel, where Brown was still searching. Brown almost proved to be a problem. He saw Bones coming and almost managed to draw his own pistol before Bones closed the distance between them.

He seized Brown's wrist before he could take hold of his weapon, then head-butted him across the bridge of the nose. He followed it up by driving a knee into his groin, which sent him crumbling to the ground. One precisely-targeted punch behind the ear and Brown was lying dazed on the ground.

Once he was disarmed and trussed, Brown offered no further resistance. He answered all of Bones' questions, though he had little more to offer than his partner. They were members of the Tuatha de Dannan who had been sent here to search for clues to the treasure, and to find out what Isla might know. They answered to someone named Brigid, whom he referred to as an elder. Bones had heard that title used before by those against whom he and Maddock had run up in the past.

"Are you connected to the Dominion?" he asked.

Brown was either an excellent actor, or he'd genuinely never heard of the organization to which Bones and Maddock had delivered a crippling blow. One which still had not been eradicated.

"No idea what you're talking about. The Tuatha are

an ancient order, and we only want what is ours."

"And you'll kill in order to get it?" Bones asked, waving the pistol he'd taken from Brown.

"We have a right to defend ourselves."

Bones smiled. "And how did that work out for you?"

Brown scowled and lapsed into silence.

Bones considered his options. He saw no need to kill these men. What did they really know, other than his face and Isla's name and description? He freed Brown's ankles and escorted him back to the castle, where he collected Isla and Campbell. From there, he led them back to their SUV, shoved them in the back, hogtied them, and locked them inside.

"Someone will find them in the morning," he said to Isla as they headed back to the castle.

"Unless the Tuatha send someone to check on them."

"I got the impression they were the only ones assigned to this detail. But, if more of the Tuatha show up, we're ready for them." Bones patted his waistband, where he had secured the two pistols he'd taken from the men.

Isla looked uncertainly at the weapons, then slowly nodded.

"All right, what do we do now?" she asked.

He took a long look out at the water and sighed. "We hope Maddock and Grizzly find something soon."

CHAPTER 18

Beneath Dunstaffnage Castle

Maddock slid downward, shooting forward at a steep angle. The beam of his headlamp bounced off a low ceiling a few feet above his head. Alongside him, Grizzly shrieked and covered his face. Ignoring him, Maddock looked down and saw that the slope ended about twenty feet ahead and braced himself for impact. They hit the ground hard, the detritus from the shattered ledge spilling around them.

"Holy crap," Maddock groaned. He took a moment to check himself for injuries. Only scrapes and bruises. Nothing broken.

"Give me a hand up?" Grizzly asked.

Maddock considered telling the man where to go, but he relented and hauled the cryptid hunter to his feet. "Are you hurt?" He didn't exactly care what happened to Grizzly, but if the man had a broken leg or some other injury that would prevent him from climbing out and making the swim back to Dunstaffnage, it would fall on Maddock to rescue him. He didn't need the inconvenience.

"I'm good. My butt's sore." Grizzly rubbed his backside for emphasis. "I guess it's because I'm a man of action. I don't sit around, so my ass isn't accustomed to making contact with hard surfaces." He forced a laugh.

Maddock clenched his fist and imagined it making contact with Grizzly's face.

"I want you to listen to me very carefully. Don't… touch… anything."

Grizzly smiled. "Relax. We're all right, aren't we? And I managed to discover…whatever this is. It's like I said, if there's a trapdoor, I'll find it."

Gritting his teeth, Maddock turned and shone his light all around.

They were in a natural cave. Moisture coated the

surface above them, which gleamed under the beams of their lights. A single stalactite, smooth and glistening, hung from the middle of the ceiling. Every few seconds, a single drop of water fell from its tip down onto an oddly shaped stalagmite, which stood at the center of a dark pool. The steady drip, along with Grizzly's labored breathing, were the only sounds.

A line of Celtic symbols—single, double, and triple spirals—led the way to the statue, which stood in the center of a triskele pattern.

As they moved closer, Maddock realized that it was not a stalagmite at all, but a statue. The steady drip of water over countless years had eroded its features. The top of its head was gone, and rivulets marred its surface. Still, he could tell the figure was female, clad in an ornate robe, and holding what had once been a bowl or a disc of some sort. A serpent lay coiled at her feet.

"That's Danu," Grizzly said. "She's the mother goddess of the Tuatha de Dannan." He reached out to touch her face, but Maddock seized his wrist.

"I told you not to touch anything."

The twinkle in Grizzly's brown eyes faded as he met the cold steel of Maddock's gaze. "It's cool." He drew away, hands held up as if he were being arrested.

Maddock stared for a few seconds longer, just to show he meant business, before continuing his inspection of the cave. Hidden in the darkness stood four large stone blocks, carved of basalt, each at one of the compass points if Maddock did not miss his guess.

"There's writing on them," Grizzly said. "Lia Fáil, Lug, Nuada, Dagda."

"What do they mean?" Maddock asked.

"Stone, spear, sword, and cauldron."

"Great." Maddock ran a hand through his hair. "It looks like the four treasures were once here." He pictured the artifacts, each on its respective pedestal, standing beneath the watchful gaze of the Tuathan goddess.

"How did they even find this place?" Grizzly asked.

"Someone without diving gear held his breath and swam into a dark underwater channel until he found this cave?"

"I have a feeling there was once a way down here from the castle, probably close to the trapdoor you so cleverly found. Whoever took the treasure, assuming it was real, and these aren't symbolic representations, must have sealed it up."

"But why seal it up once the treasure was gone?"

"To cover their tracks, I suppose," Maddock said. "If knowledge of this place came to light, people might start believing the treasures are more than a mere legend."

"I think this proves the treasures are real," Grizzly said. "If they were figurative, there wouldn't be a simple stone block with the words on them."

Maddock nodded. "They'd have carved representations of the treasures, just like they made the image of their goddess." It felt odd to agree with Grizzly, but at least the man wasn't a complete idiot.

"The million-dollar question is where did they go?" Grizzly said.

"There's got to be a clue," Maddock said.

"How do you figure?"

"I've seen it more times than I can count. When something sacred is moved to a new location, there's always someone who is so afraid of it being lost forever, that they leave a message behind just in case."

"What about when an enemy takes it?" Grizzly asked. "Like when the Babylonians took the Ark of the Covenant?"

Maddock could have told him a few things about the sacred ark, but he kept his knowledge to himself. "Depends. In a situation like you describe, they'll often leave a gloating message behind. Usually, something like that isn't kept a secret. They want the world to know they've taken the enemy's most treasured possessions."

"Like a Roman triumph, when they'd parade the treasures of the conquered nation to show off the fruits of their victory."

"Exactly." Again, Maddock felt a twinge of discomfort at agreeing with Grizzly. "What we need to do now is look for such a message."

"I'll keep my fingers crossed." Grizzly gave him a wink. "And I promise not to touch anything."

They gave the cavern a thorough, floor-to-ceiling search, but found nothing. Maddock had hoped that one of the pedestals on which the treasure once stood might hold a clue, but they were free of any markings aside from the names of the treasures.

"Maybe there was a clue, but it got eroded away?" Grizzly asked.

Eroded! Maddock returned to the statue of Danu. If anything had been washed away, this would be the most likely place.

"Do you see something?" Grizzly asked.

"Help me look." He examined every inch of the statue, from head to toe. And then his gaze drifted to the serpent at her feet, and something caught his eye. What he'd initially taken to be the snake's faded markings were, in fact, a series of symbols scraped into the stone. "I think this is it!" He took out his camera and began photographing the markings. "Jimmy's going to kill me when I ask him to decipher this."

"Isla has a friend—a codebreaker by the name of Meikle. He helped us with the last clue. He'd probably help with this one, too."

"Works for me. Two heads are better than one." Maddock barked a rueful laugh. "These people do like their puzzles, don't they?"

CHAPTER 19

Edinburgh, Scotland

Walter Meikle sat in a high-backed chair, feet propped up, thumbing absently through an aged volume of Tuatha mythology. The yellowed pages made a pleasant scratching sound as he slowly turned them. He looked at each word but digested only a few. He turned another page and stopped at a detailed, black and white image of the goddess Danu. He knew it was merely his imagination, but it seemed accusation shone in her eyes as she gazed up at him. He snapped the book closed and tossed it on the table beside him, knocking over his empty teacup in the process.

"Damn," he muttered.

His phone rang, and he stared at the name for a full three seconds before answering. Isla Mulheron. Why couldn't the girl just leave it alone? But he knew the answer, knew she would not relent.

"Hello?"

"Meikle? It's Isla Mulheron. Listen, the Dunstaffnage clue was spot-on."

"Really?" Meikle sat up straight. "What did you find?" He felt his eyes go wide as she described an underwater passageway, a trapdoor, and a treasure room hidden in a cave far beneath the castle.

"And you're confident the treasures were once kept there?" His reservations about her, his wishes for her to leave him alone, were forgotten.

"As certain as we can be."

Meikle squeezed the phone, tension knotting his back. "Did you…run into any trouble? The passageway and cave were structurally sound, I mean," he hastily added, not wanting to rouse her suspicion.

"I didn't go down with them. SCUBA isn't my thing. But the guys who went in made it back okay."

"Guys? I thought it was only you and

that…interesting fellow."

Isla let out a long sigh. "You noticed. Believe me, he wasn't my first choice of partners. But yes, we've added a couple more to our team. Capable men, unlike Grizzly."

Meikle breathed a sigh of relief. He'd hated reporting Isla's first clue to the Tuatha, but he'd had no choice. He had feared for her safety, but it appeared they'd made contact with Isla and managed to bring her into the fold, or at least convince her they were on the same side. This also meant that he was not in trouble for concealing her identity. That was a tremendous weight off his shoulders.

"The reason I'm calling is, I need your help again."

"Oh?"

"We found a set of symbols that had apparently been added to the Danu statue well after its installation. We believe it's a code or cipher of some sort, but you'd know for sure."

Meikle's heart raced. If she was correct, they were finally on the path laid down for the worthy. The treasure might finally be within reach. He'd waited all his life for such a breakthrough.

"Send it along. I'll see what I can do."

"Will do. Please let me know as soon as you come up with something."

Meikle forced a laugh. "I appreciate your confidence in me. It could take time, but I'll keep you posted." He bade her goodbye and immediately headed to his computer.

By the time he'd logged in and opened his email server, he had multiple emails from Isla, each with a pair of high-resolution photographs attached. His breath caught in his chest as he clicked through them. A stone serpent slithered across his monitor, and then a series of close-up photos showing symbols that appeared to have been scraped out with a knife.

"Oh, my dear," he said. "What have you found?"

CHAPTER 20

Oban, Scotland

Maddock listened intently, his ale forgotten as Isla discussed their find with her friend, Meikle. Though his attention was focused on her conversation, he kept his eyes turned away, gazing out the window at the dark blue waters of the Firth of Lorn. A small resort town near Dunstaffnage Castle, Oban was picturesque, but the view left him cold on the inside.

He turned his attention to Bones' and Grizzly's discussion of Bigfoot. The two were getting along famously, but Isla seemed to share Maddock's low opinion of the cryptid hunter.

"You and I should go Bigfoot hunting sometime," Grizzly said to Bones. "Unless you'd rather stay close to home and look for the Skunk Ape instead."

"Bigfoot would be cool," Bones said hurriedly. He flashed a knowing glance in Maddock's direction.

"Meikle says it could take some time," Isla said, pocketing her phone.

"If he manages to decipher it at all," Grizzly added.

"You've seen him in action. If anyone can do it, he can," she said.

"It's a race, then," Maddock said. "Our hacker versus your scholar."

"Let's make it a bet," Bones said. "Loser buys dinner and drinks...and pays for the hotel room." He gave Isla a wink.

"Fine by me," Isla said. "As long as you bunk with Grizzly."

"Hey now!" Grizzly said, laughing. "Don't I get a say in this?"

"No." Isla turned and smiled at Maddock. He felt his cheeks flush and he quickly raised his ale and took a long swig.

"Slow it down," she said. "I'm not trying to get you

drunk."

Maddock tried to think of a clever repartee, but that was Bones' specialty, not that most of Bones' comments were particularly clever.

"Actually, I have to make a call. If you'll excuse me?" He stood up too fast and banged his knee on the table, nearly upsetting everyone's drinks.

"Time to cut you off, Maddock," Bones said.

"Maybe." He made his way out of the pub and onto the street. The sidewalks bustled with tourists selecting a lunchtime destination. The aroma of seafood blended with the damp breeze blowing in off the water. He found a relatively quiet spot and called Angel.

The conversation was brief. He gave her the broad strokes of their latest mystery, omitting the men they'd encountered the previous day. Angel said all the right things, but she didn't ask her usual dozen questions, didn't say how much she wished she were there. She told him about her new agent, who had apparently been showing her all the sights in introducing her to all the interesting people in Hollywood. He ended the conversation before they hit the long silence that seemed to plague most of their recent talks.

As he made his way back to the restaurant, he checked his email and was pleased to see he had a message from Colin Jeong. He scanned it and grinned.

"Bones is going to love this," he said to no one in particular.

Their meals had arrived by the time he returned to the table. As he dug into a dish of mussels, scallops and crab rillettes, he filled the others in on Jeong's findings.

"He says the tooth is genuine and it's definitely no more than one hundred fifty years old."

"As if we didn't know that already," Bones said.

Maddock ignored him. "The creature it came from comes from Scotland and its diet consisted of eels, salmon, and seals."

"How could he tell that?" Isla asked.

"Something called 'stable isotope analysis.'"

"Yep. Stable isotope analysis," Grizzly said, nodding. "That's what I figured."

"Really?" Maddock asked. "How does it work? Jeong didn't elaborate in his email."

"I, um," Grizzly shoveled a chunk of lobster in his mouth and chewed slowly, his face growing ever redder under Maddock's and Isla's twin stares. "It's too much to explain. It wouldn't make any sense if you weren't already familiar with the scientific underpinnings of the process."

"Sure. Anyway, he wants to do further testing on it. He said it would require taking a part of the tooth. I told him that was all right by me. We need the information more than we need a tooth no one will believe isn't a forgery."

"So we're looking for a body of water in Scotland where you can find seals, eels, and salmon," Bones said. "That narrows it down a bit."

"There's one more thing he mentioned," Maddock said. "The tooth definitely came from a plesiosaur."

Grizzly and Bones let out whoops of excitement.

Isla looked from the two men to Maddock. "Seriously? You want to go there?"

"We need something to do while we're waiting for one of our guys to break the code. And there's one place above all others that fits the bill."

"Look at them. They're like little kids at Christmas," she said, inclining her head toward Bones and Grizzly, who were high-fiving.

"True, but I can't bring myself to disappoint Bones. He's wanted to go there forever."

"This," Isla said, "is going to be one long drive."

CHAPTER 21

Urquhart Castle, Loch Ness

The ruins of Urquhart Castle stood on the banks of Loch Ness in the midst of the picturesque Scottish Highlands. Dating from the thirteenth to sixteenth centuries, the iconic castle was perhaps the best-known site associated with Loch Ness. Built on the site of a medieval fort, Urquhart had served as a royal castle until a series of raids took its toll. Now, little remained of its former grandeur.

Maddock found it difficult to believe he was actually seeing it in person. His was not the joyous, wide-eyed stare with which Bones took in the crumbling walls of the upper and nether baileys, the remains of the great hall, and the grandeur of Grant's Tower, which graced most Loch Ness postcards. He did, however, feel a sense of completion as he checked off this bucket list item.

He paused, staring out at the dark, serene waters of the legendary Scottish lake, and let the atmosphere wash over him. Growing up, he'd been fascinated by the legend of Nessie, the monster of the loch. Over time, he'd come to believe her a myth, one kept alive by the tourist industry that had grown up around Loch Ness. Nothing he'd seen since their arrival that morning had changed his mind, at least on the latter score. But with the discovery of the tooth, he at least had to consider the possibility.

Isla sidled up to him. "I don't know about this, Maddock. So much of the Nessie story is utter bollocks."

A group of tourists standing nearby cast baleful stares in their direction.

"Not a popular opinion around here," he said. "Maybe mind your volume?" He added a wink to show he was joking.

"But surely you know all the objections?" She began

counting on her fingers as she enumerated her concerns. "Putting aside some of the hoaxes, there's the lack of food supply to support a breeding population; the utter improbability of a prehistoric creature living here for God knows how long without a single, fully verifiable sighting; no scientific evidence; and no carcasses washing ashore. Nothing. And in an age where everyone has a phone with a camera, why aren't we getting new pictures of her?"

"You've been listening to the wrong people." Grizzly had overheard their conversation, and he and Bones moved to flank Maddock and Isla. "Nessie sightings are actually on the rise. There have been several in the past couple of years, and we're not talking about drunkards or crackpots."

"No, just tourists who are desperate to catch a glimpse of a monster. That and true believers who jump at every piece of floating debris."

"Come on, chick. Don't be a cynic," Bones said. "It's not impossible that some sort of creature lives primarily in the sea, but comes here from time to time."

Isla rounded on Bones. "And gets here how? Splashing along the River Ness, right through the heart of Inverness?"

"Saint Columba spotted her in the River Ness," Grizzly said.

"Whatever. I just don't believe she could traverse the river without being seen several times."

"She, or they, wouldn't come by river," Bones said. "They'd come by underwater channels that eventually lead to the sea."

Isla rolled her eyes and let out a huff of breath.

"It's not impossible," Bones went on. "Non-native shells have been found in the Loch. And let's be real—no one's ever done a serious exploration of every nook and cranny of this place. It's too big, too many cracks and crevasses, and visibility is awful."

"Let's say I believe there are such channels. We're talking about a creature moving from salt water to fresh water and back."

"Saltwater crocs," Grizzly offered.

"Bull sharks," Bones chimed in.

Isla turned pleading eyes at Maddock. "Help me."

Maddock laughed. "You got yourself into this. Over the past several years, I've learned to keep a check on my skepticism, or at least try."

"Fine." She turned back to Bones and Grizzly. "I can accept that at least some of the monster sightings are living creatures, and not just logs, gas bubbles, or hoaxes. But a prehistoric creature?"

"What is it, then?" Grizzly asked.

"Seals, giant eels, perhaps Wels catfish."

Bones snorted. "Catfish? Come on. Have you heard of Operation Deepscan? They turned up a bunch of hits on large, unknown creatures. And another expedition got underwater photos of massive flippers and one of a long-necked creature."

"Blurry, photographically enhanced images," Isla said.

"Only because the water's so clogged with peat particles that a better image is impossible," Grizzly said.

Maddock had heard enough. "Look, we aren't going to settle this. The fact of the matter is, we found an actual tooth from a plesiosaur that lived in the Irish Sea a little over a century ago. That proves that a sea creature *can* go undiscovered for thousands upon thousands of years."

"Coelacanth," Bones harrumphed, covering a fake cough.

Maddock shot a reproving glance at him. "And while that doesn't mean similar creatures lived in this loch, it's worth checking out."

Isla gave a reluctant nod. "All right. But can we agree there's no way a German U-boat could have made its way to the Loch?"

Maddock raised his hand to forestall arguments from Bones and Grizzly. "Let's agree it's unlikely."

A sudden uproar from a group of tourists drew their attention.

Maddock whipped his head around, his senses on high alert since the events of the previous day.

"Oh my God! What is that?" A young woman pointed out into the loch.

Maddock's jaw dropped when he saw what she was looking at. A row of low, dark humps was slicing through the water, making its way down the middle of the loch.

People shouted with excitement. Camera shutters clicked. Phones and tablets were trained on the moving object.

For a moment, Maddock was a true believer. He raised his camera and focused on the row of humps.

And then it was gone, followed down into the water by a chorus of groans from the onlookers.

"False alarm." Disappointment hung heavy on Bones' words.

"What do you mean?" Isla asked. The sparkle in her eyes said she, too, was beginning to forget her skepticism.

"It's a common phenomenon in lakes, particularly a narrow one like this," Bones said, gazing at the spot where the humps had melted away.

"A boat comes by, and its wake spreads out in both directions," Grizzly said, picking up the explanation. "Eventually the waves created by the boat bounce off the sides of the Loch and move back toward the center. Sometimes you don't even see them until they collide again, long after the boat is gone."

"And the collision creates what looks like a series of humps," Bones said.

Maddock understood. "And gives the illusion of movement. That's disappointing."

"Enough excitement for now," Isla said. "Let's proceed with the treasure hunt. There's a tour group over there." She inclined her head toward Grant's Tower. "Maddock and I will speak with the tour guide. See if he knows any legends of treasure around here."

Bones quirked an eyebrow. "Why just you and

Maddock?"

"You're too intimidating," she said. "The guy might be hesitant to talk if you're looking over him."

"People say that about me, too," Grizzly said. "It's frustrating."

"Sure. How about you and Bones take another look around the ruins for any signs of the Tuatha? Symbols we missed. Carvings and the like."

The two nodded, though Maddock thought he saw a touch of suspicion in Bones' eyes. He made a point to keep a respectful distance from Isla as they walked away.

The tour guide was a tall, fair-skinned man with a thick head of white hair and twinkling blue eyes. His name tag read "Douglas." He greeted them warmly and was happy to chat about the history of the castle and Nessie sightings that had occurred in this area. When Maddock steered the conversation toward the topic of treasure, he raised his bushy eyebrows in surprise.

"You're the first to ask me about the Urquhart Treasure. It's not commonly-known."

"We actually don't know anything about it," Isla said. "I'm writing a book on legendary Scottish treasures and wondered about any that might be associated with the Loch."

"Well then," Douglas said. "You'll be wanting to know about the Urquhart Treasure, I suppose Long ago, Highlanders called this place Strone Castle, after the fortress that sat here upon Strone Point. As legend had it, the old fortress that sat here was built atop two vaulted cells built into the hollow rock below. One of the cells is filled with gold—a treasure of unimaginable value. The other seals up a pestilence that, if it were released, could wipe out all of Scotland. And no one knows which vault is which, save the men who sealed them there long ago, and that secret died with them."

"The Lady or the Tiger?" Isla said.

"Exactly," Douglas agreed. "Even if someone found the treasure, they'd have to be certain which vault they were opening, or else all could be lost. Assuming one believes the legend is true, that is."

"Has anyone ever searched for the treasure?" Maddock asked.

Douglas shook his head. "Not as far as I know. As I told you, it's not very well-known, and the few who know about it take it none too serious."

"Any chambers underneath the ruins?" Maddock pressed

"Not that anyone's found. Given that, in its long history, the castle has been raided, pillaged, and even blown up, if there are vaults down there, they're buried deep. Of course, the water level of the Loch has risen quite a bit since the construction of the Caledonian Canal back in the 1800s. Perhaps there's a way in from under the water."

"Any idea who put the treasure there? The Tuatha de Dannan perhaps?" Isla asked.

Douglas' smile melted. "No idea. If you'll excuse me, I'll be getting back to my group now."

"That was odd," Isla whispered.

"Yeah. Considering the guys who tried to kidnap you are Tuatha, you should probably keep mention of them on the down-low."

"All right." She sighed, stared down at her hands. "It's certainly not the Tuatha I imagined when mum and dad used to tell me stories as a child."

Maddock looked at Isla. Something had been bothering him since they'd first met.

"Isla, you mentioned your parents. You said they 'believed' in the treasure. What did you mean by that?"

"They're dead," she said flatly. The expression on her face said no further questions would be welcome.

Maddock considered pressing the issue, but then his phone vibrated. He checked it to find a message from Jimmy.

Check your email. Found the key in a scan of an old journal. I'm not saying where I had to hack into in order to find it. You owe me bigger than ever.

Maddock smiled and texted back. *You live for this*

stuff. He laughed aloud when Jimmy immediately replied with a photo of Johnny Cash giving the finger to the camera.

"Good news?" Isla asked.

"I think so." He opened his email and gave it a quick read. "Looks like our guy wins."

"Seriously?"

He handed her the phone and she read Jimmy's email with interest. "Mind if I pass this along to Meikle? Perhaps he could reverse engineer it for confirmation."

Maddock shrugged. "Can't hurt. Two heads are better than one."

While they headed off in search of Bones and Grizzly, Isla called Meikle and shared with him the message Jimmy had decoded. He expressed surprise that someone had decoded the message so quickly, but promised to do what he could to confirm it.

They found Bones and Grizzly down by the waterfront. Grizzly was loudly speculating about the possibilities of a dive in this area.

"I think we should scour it thoroughly. No one with my level of experience has ever..." He halted in midsentence when he saw Maddock.

Maddock figured he'd hold off on mentioning the legend of the treasure since they now had a new lead to follow. He didn't need to fuel Grizzly's desire to make another dive. Any more underwater exploits would be himself and Bones.

"We totally struck out. No signs of the Tuatha anywhere," Bones said. "How about you? Did you get lucky?"

Maddock didn't miss the double-entendre, but he chose to ignore it. "We might have. Jimmy thinks he's deciphered the clue from Dunstaffnage."

"Hell, yes!" Bones pumped his fist. "What is it?"

"We need to find a place called the Well of the Dead."

CHAPTER 22

Culloden Battlefield

The sign up ahead read Culloden Battlefield. Maddock looked out across the rolling, green landscape, heart racing as it always did when he was hot on the trail of a treasure. The historic battlefield, the site of the final battle of the Jacobite rebellion of 1745, stood only a short distance east of Inverness, very close to Loch Ness.

"Tell me again exactly how the message reads," Isla said.

"Beneath the Well of the Dead, Saint Columba's beastie guards the treasure from the unworthy." Maddock had memorized it by now.

"The only Well of the Dead I've ever heard of is here at the battlefield," she said. "Internet searches didn't come up with anything else, so fingers crossed."

"The Saint Columba bit is a home run," Grizzly said.

Isla glanced at him through the rearview mirror. "You guys mentioned that name earlier. What's the story, again?"

Bones cleared his throat loudly and affected a lecturing tone. "Saint Columba was a traveling monk. Back in the sixth century..."

"565 AD," Grizzly interjected.

"Not important to the story, but okay. Back in 565, he was traveling in the area of Loch Ness when he came across some locals..."

"Picts," Grizzly said.

"Maybe you could have him tell the story. He seems to know it better than you do," Maddock jibed.

"He doesn't know it at all. He's got an article open on his phone and he's injecting superfluous details."

Grizzly smiled. "The women say I make everything super."

Bones gave him a long, blank stare. "Dude, I have no

freaking idea if you're joking or not. Anyway, Saint Columba came across a group of *Picts* on the shore of the River Ness who were burying one of their own. They told him the man had been bitten by a water monster that terrorized them from time to time. They were able to catch him with hooks and lines and pull him to shore before he was devoured, but they didn't manage to save him." He paused and looked at Grizzly, as if daring him to interrupt, before continuing his story. "Saint Columba needed to get across the river, and there was a boat on the other side. Either he didn't believe the story about the monster or he was kind of a tool, because he made one of his men swim across to retrieve the boat."

"Big mistake," Grizzly said.

This time, Bones ignored him. "So, the dude gets out into the water and, big surprise, here comes the monster. Saint Columba raises his staff, calls up some Jesus mojo, and tells the monster to walk, which he does."

"Some stories also say he used his staff to raise the dead man," Grizzly added, "but they aren't considered reliable."

"But the monster story *is* considered reliable?" Isla asked, eyebrows raised.

"We're not going to go through this all over again, are we?" Bones said.

"I suppose not," Isla said. "So it does seem to connect with the tooth and the Loch Ness legend. And if there truly are underwater channels leading from the loch to the sea, it's not unreasonable to think one might run beneath Culloden."

"That's what I like to hear," Bones said. "It doesn't hurt to put your skepticism on the back burner every once in a while. About a lot of things," he added with a sly wink.

"If you say so," Isla said. "Understand, the only reason I'm even entertaining this notion is the fact that you guys recovered that tooth. And even that I'm taking on faith, since all I've seen are photos."

"Just to be clear," Bones said, "*I* found the tooth.

Maddock just came along for the swim."

"Yeah, but who found the journal?" Maddock retorted, then immediately kicked himself for stooping to Bones' level.

"Fine. You're both very talented." Isla reached over and patted Maddock's thigh. He didn't miss how long her hand lingered there before she removed it.

They parked the car in the lot closest to the Well of the Dead and began the short walk to the site. They hadn't gone far when Isla let out an audible gasp.

"What is it?" Maddock asked.

"Looks like the Tuatha got here first." She pointed to a group of four standing a hundred or so yards ahead of them. "You see the tall man with the long gray hair? That's Michael Fairly, an old friend of my father. He's obsessed with the history and legends of the Tuatha de Dannan. On more than one occasion, Dad hinted that Michael was one of them."

"What about the others?" Maddock asked.

Isla squinted. "I can't tell. It's too far and they're all facing away. None of them look familiar."

As they watched, one man slowly turned around.

"Unless I'm mistaken," Bones said, "the guy on the far right is Brown, one of the guys I caught at Dunstaffnage."

"You've got sharp eyes," Isla said.

"That's only one of the many services I provide," Bones said. "By the way, at least one of them is a woman. She's wearing a suit, but it's definitely a chick. Can't tell about the other."

"What do we do?" Isla asked.

"I don't want a confrontation if we can help it," Maddock said. "Bones and I have two pistols and sixteen bullets between us. We should assume all of them are armed, and that they have backup in the area."

"I'm a good shot if you want me to take one of the guns," Grizzly offered.

"I don't," Maddock said. "You guys go back to the car. I'll see if I can sneak up on them. If they find something down there, we might have to take steps. If it proves to be a dead end, they'll have done our work for us."

"I'm better at blending into the landscape," Bones said.

"That's debatable, and in Scotland, you stand out a lot more than I do. Hell, you stand out anywhere. Now, let's move before they see us."

Maddock made a quick sprint for the nearby tree line. The forest was sparse but provided sufficient coverage for one as experienced as he was at hiding behind cover. He quickly closed the distance between himself and the four members of the Tuatha, and shadowed them until he ran out of forest. He watched as the group stopped at a stone marker. He knew from photographs that this was the site of the Well of the Dead.

Lush grass, knee high in places, ran from the forest to the well. "I guess it's basic training all over again," Maddock said. He chose his spot with care, dropped to the ground, and crawled forward until he was within earshot of the foursome. A low stone wall, buried in the same deep grass, stood between Maddock and the Tuatha, and ran all the way down to the small pool of water that was the well itself. If Maddock wanted to, he could crawl within arm's reach of it unseen. At the moment, there didn't seem to be any need to get closer.

He peered through the lush greenery, and managed to get a good look at his quarry. Fairly, the gray-haired man whom Isla had identified as a friend of her father, stood with his hands on his hips, looking down at the stone marker. Brown stood twenty paces away, staring out at the parking lot. Maddock could tell by the lump inside the man's jacket pocket that he'd replaced the weapon Bones had taken from him. The other two were middle-aged, one a tall and distinguished-looking woman with gray-streaked auburn hair, knotted in a bun. The other was a rail-thin woman with short, red hair and a permanent scowl. Both wore expensive-looking suits, tailor made by Maddock's estimation.

His eyes moved to the triangular stone marker at the edge of the pathway that ended at the well. A message was engraved in the surface in rough text:

WELL OF THE DEAD

HERE THE CHIEF OF THE MACGILLIVRAYS FELL

The Tuatha stared at the marker, then moved along to the small pool.

"I don't see how this could possibly be the place," Fairly said. "I've checked the geological surveys and there's nothing down there. I think this is a dead end."

Maddock had to agree. The Well of the Dead was not his idea of a well. It was just a very small hole from which water bubbled up. Back in the states it would have been called a natural spring.

"I thought you said your man, Meikle, was reliable," the older woman said.

Maddock's fists clenched at the mention of Isla's friend. Rather, the man she thought was a friend. So that's how the Tuatha had managed to dog their trail.

"Brigid, we've been through this," Fairly said. "Meikle is competent and dependable, but there are bound to be occasional mistakes in his work. He's decrypting codes that have withstood translation for years, centuries even. Sometimes there's a certain amount of guesswork involved."

Brigid rubbed her chin, nodding thoughtfully. "He was correct about Dunstaffnage. And no one would have suspected the existence of the cavern found by Isla and her people. Perhaps this is a similar situation?"

"You mean there's a cavern deep underground?" Fairly gave a shake of the head. "I doubt it."

"We should have the area excavated, just to be safe. Or at least drill down and check for open spaces."

"That could be a problem," Fairly said.

Brigid quirked an eyebrow. "Not for me." She took out his phone, but before she could punch up a number, Brown hurried forward.

"I apologize for the interruption," he said quickly. "I think there's a problem."

Brigid froze, slowly raised her head. "Go on," she said, not looking at Brown.

"I just saw the big Indian who…"

"The man who single-handedly neutralized you and Campbell?"

At that, the thin, red-haired woman let out a harsh laugh.

"Where did you see him?" Brigid asked.

"In the car park. I couldn't tell who else his is with him, but I assume one of them is," he hesitated, "Isla Mulheron." He swallowed hard. "What do you want me to do?"

Brigid exhaled slowly. "Isla is here, which means we are no longer one step behind her. Her companions can safely be eliminated." She turned to the red-haired woman. "O'Brien, go with him and make sure he doesn't make a botch of it. And no witnesses."

O'Brien drew her pistol and grinned.

"I can do it," Brown said hurriedly. "Please let me take care of it."

Brigid looked at Fairly, who nodded.

"We don't know how many men she has in her employ. Campbell's sweeping the area, but he could be a long way away. It might be a good idea to keep O'Brien with us."

Brigid finally looked in Brown's direction. "Fine. Make it quick and clean."

Heart racing, Maddock took out his phone and fired off a quick text message to Bones.

Tuatha coming. Get out of here.

The reply came a few seconds later.

Roger that. What about you?

Maddock tapped a quick reply.

I'll catch up.

He put away his phone and assessed the situation. He was confident there was nothing to be found here at the well. Either Jimmy had made a mistake in the translation or the clue was a false lead. He had a pistol with eight shots. Brigid and Fairly were completely unaware of his presence, but now that they knew Bones was in the area, O'Brien appeared to be on high alert. She still had her weapon drawn, and her eyes swept the grassy area where Maddock was concealed.

Maddock had no idea of O'Brien's level of skill, nor how close by Campbell might be. It was too risky to try and take all three of them out. Besides that, Maddock was no assassin. Yes, Brigid had ordered Brown to eliminate Bones and Grizzly, but none of the people standing before him posed an immediate threat to Maddock. The rationalizing required to turn three murders into an act of self-defense was too much for him. He'd simply have to get away.

Moving silent as a snake in tall grass, he dropped onto his belly and slithered away.

I hope I don't end up regretting this.

A ghostly air seemed to hang around the Clava Cairns. The Bronze Age cemetery complex lay a little over a mile from Culloden, but it felt worlds away. A complex array of graves, cairns, and standing stones gave it an unearthly feel. As Maddock emerged from the trees and into their midst, he almost expected to be greeted by the ghosts of long-dead soldiers.

He'd had no difficulty getting away from the unsuspecting members of the Tuatha, who were focused on plotting their next move. None of them believed the Well of the Dead would turn up any new clues, and seemed at a loss for where to go next. The problem was, Maddock and his friends were at a similar standstill.

"At least we're not running behind," he said.

A pair of tourists passed by. He greeted them with a smile and a nod, and was taken aback when they frowned and hurried away. It took him a moment to realize what had elicited the reaction. His clothing was filthy, streaked with mud and covered in grass stains and dirt smudges from his crawl through the grass.

"Smooth as ever, Maddock." Bones appeared from behind a tree that Maddock swore wasn't large enough to hide his friend's bulk. "You charm everyone you meet."

"You got away all right?" Maddock asked.

"No problem at all," Bones said. "There were only a couple of cars in the parking lot besides ours. I figured one or both belonged to the Tuatha, so I slashed their tires."

"Nice. Where are Isla and Grizzly?"

"Over there." He inclined his head toward one of the ring cairns.

The low, round structure loomed atop a large earth mound. The cairn itself stood shoulder height to Maddock. The base was constructed of huge, gray stones. The center was filled in with stones of varying sizes. A slit just wide enough for a man to walk through radiated out from an open ring in the center. Inside, Grizzly and Isla waited.

"What's the situation?" Isla asked. "Have the Tuatha found anything yet?"

Maddock filled them in on what he had seen and heard. Isla expressed shock and anger at Meikle's betrayal.

"Have you heard of this Brigid person? Any idea who she is?"

Isla flinched at the name.

"You know her," Maddock said.

"No. It's actually a common first name." Her eyes took on a faraway look. "You know how, sometimes, you hear a name and it reminds you of someone you'd rather not think about?"

"Jade," Bones piped up.

"Screw you, Bones," Maddock said.

"Brigid was a goddess and a member of the Tuatha de Danann. She was the daughter of the Dagda, the god who was closely associated with the cauldron. I grew up hearing all about her from my parents."

"She apparently wields some serious power. She

seems to think she has enough clout to actually excavate around the well, right in the middle of an important historical site. Of course, she thinks it's a dead end. Just wants to leave no stone unturned," Maddock concluded.

"I think I agree with her," Isla said. "Based on the photos of the Well of the Dead, I suspected this was the wrong place."

"That's what we thought about Dunstaffnage until I found the underground chamber," Grizzly said.

"Finding something and falling through a trapdoor aren't exactly the same thing," Bones said.

Grizzly looked like he was about to argue the point, but Maddock cut him off.

"We need to focus on our next move. Maybe there's another Well of the Dead somewhere?"

"It's possible," Isla said. "Do you think Jimmy could have made a mistake?"

"Maybe, but he's pretty good."

"We need to get the Tuatha off our backs until we know where to go next. Any ideas on how to do that?" Bones asked.

Maddock looked around, as if the answer stood somewhere nearby. And then it hit him.

"As a matter of fact, I have the perfect idea."

CHAPTER 23

Loch Ness

A loud knock at her door made Isla jump. She'd been on edge ever since they'd taken rooms at the small inn near Loch Ness. She stared balefully at the door for a full five seconds, trying to decide if she hoped it was Grizzly or the Tuatha de Dannan on the other side. Neither appealed to her right now. The knock came again.

"It's me."

"Coming." She closed her laptop, stalked to the door, and flung it open.

Grizzly stood there, smiling and holding two bottles of ale.

"Thought you could use a drink," he said.

"As a matter of fact, I could." She accepted one of the bottles and returned to the small desk that occupied most of the space that her bed did not. She sat down and stared out the window at the dark waters of Loch Ness in the distance. She wondered how Maddock and Bones were making out. *They'll be fine,* she thought.

Grizzly sat down on the corner of her bed and let out a long, dramatic sigh. "I wish they had me go," he said. "I did stumble across the chamber at Dunstaffnage. I'm lucky like that. Maybe I could be of some help with the search."

"Believe me, I wish you'd gone too," Isla said through gritted teeth. She turned her back on the treasure hunter, opened her laptop, and logged back on. Once again, the photos Maddock had taken beneath Dunstaffnage filled the screen.

"I hope they don't get lost," Grizzly said. "That's a long way to swim."

"They'll be fine. They dive for a living," she said.

Not wanting to risk being spotted nosing around Urquhart Castle after hours, the two former Navy SEALs had begun their swim in a secluded area north of the ruins. The deep, steep-sided Loch provided the perfect cover. They'd be able to dive deep enough to go unseen, hugging the shore until they reached the castle. None of them held out much hope that the treasure chambers beneath the castle were more than a legend, but they were stuck for the moment, so any avenue was worth exploring.

Meanwhile, Maddock's hacker friend had curtly reminded them that he did have a day job, but promised to take a second look at the cipher as soon as he had a chance.

"I wish there was something I could do to help," Grizzly said. "You need any assistance with your cipher project?"

Isla shook her head. She was already deep in thought on how to proceed on that score, and she seriously doubted Grizzly would have anything to offer.

Maddock's plan was clever, if they could pull it off. Jimmy had sent them the key to the cipher. At least, what he believed was the key. Isla would use it to create a false clue which she would send to Meikle, requesting help with another translation. With any luck, they would send the Tuatha off on a wild goose chase while she and her companions continued their pursuit of the real treasure.

But what would happen should they find it? Her editor was expecting a story, or series, about the hunt. That was no problem. She could submit any story she liked, one that would end in failure.

Grizzly would want to televise the whole thing. That wasn't acceptable by any stretch. She'd have to figure something out there. But what about Maddock? Could she make him understand what the treasure meant? What had to happen next?

She let out a long sigh. She could do nothing about that right now. She returned her thoughts to the false clue.

"The message that Maddock found beneath Dunstaffnage… the message *you* and Maddock found, that is," she added hurriedly, "contains almost all the letters in the alphabet. There are only seven for which I don't have symbols. Avoiding those letters, I've put together a new message. I've also made a slight alteration to the vowels. Not enough, hopefully, that it will stump Meikle, but sufficient to make it seem like we believe this to be a new code."

"Let's hear it," Grizzly said.

"The worthy must brave the demon of Borthwick to claim the treasure."

Grizzly scratched his head. "What is a Borthwick?"

"It's a haunted castle southwest of Edinburgh."

"I thought we agreed to send them to Morar," Grizzly said. "That would be more believable since they have their own lake monster, Morag."

"No, *you* wanted to send them there. There are two problems with Morar. The first is that it's too close to Loch Ness. We want their attention focused on somewhere far away."

"What's the second issue?"

She rubbed her temples, trying to fend off the oncoming headache. "Morag is the problem. The strong association with a lake monster legend means there's a chance we could end up searching there."

"Gotcha. Sounds like you've got it under control."

"I think so. The message itself is solid. It's the image I'm going to send him that worries me."

Grizzly stood and moved behind her chair. "Let's see what you've got."

She grimaced. Increasingly, she found the man's presence discomfiting. Perhaps it was the contrast to Maddock, whom she found a steadying presence. And then there was Bones, who could be a pain in his own way, but he seemed to be reliable, and Maddock trusted him utterly.

"It's my photo manipulation I'm worried about. I'm going to tell Meikle we found a cave near the well and that this was carved on a stone there. The problem is the quality of some of Maddock's photos." She clicked on one of the photographs. "See how the flash partially obscures this symbol? I think it's a combination of the moisture and the shape of the stone. If I plug this bit in, it's going to look wrong."

"I took a few pics with my phone. Maybe some of mine are better." A few seconds later, Grizzly handed her his phone. Sure enough, he had a crystal clear image of the problematic section.

"This is perfect," she said. "I'll just…" Her voice trailed off as she realized what she was looking at.

"Something wrong?"

"It's the photo you took," she said. "There are more symbols here." She grinned. "Jimmy didn't have the entire clue."

CHAPTER 24

Loch Ness

The murky waters of Loch Ness seemed to close in around Maddock as he swam in the darkness. The peat particles that filled the loch limited visibility to a few feet in front of him. It reminded him uncomfortably of clouds of silt that could blind a diver inside a sunken ship or underwater cavern. He'd long been aware of the challenges inherent in diving in the loch, but experiencing it firsthand was something else entirely. Now, as he propelled himself through the murky depths, he could easily understand how a creature could go undiscovered within these waters.

He swam along, his headlamp fighting a losing battle against the darkness that enveloped them. Something shot past them, a large silvery fish, a salmon perhaps. He didn't startle easy, but this strange place had him unnerved. Visions of the tooth he'd recovered from the U-boat kept flashing through his mind. What if the legends were true? What if they were swimming into the creature's den?

He and Bones hugged the steep, rocky side of the loch and relied on GPS to track their movements. When they'd reached the area below Urquhart Castle, he signaled to Bones, and they began their search.

Careful to shield their lamps, they began just below the surface of the lake, and quickly worked their way down. Maddock swam back and forth, his eyes searching the shadows, looking for anything that might indicate a passageway leading beneath the castle.

Fifteen minutes later, their search hadn't turned up anything. Bones gave a shake of his head and turned his thumb down. He hated thorough searches. If luck didn't lead him to the prize in short order, he grew impatient and annoying, though he stuck to the task until the end.

Maddock checked his dive watch and held up ten

fingers. If they didn't find anything within ten minutes, they'd give it up. Bones nodded and they continued their search.

As they swam, Maddock found his thoughts drifting. If this dive proved fruitless, what would they do next? Call it quits? No, he couldn't do that. He wasn't one to give up on a treasure hunt, and he couldn't let Isla down. She'd confided in him how important this treasure hunt was to her. Her family... *Stop thinking about Isla,* he chided himself.

He didn't think about the beautiful journalist for long. As he swam into a dark crevasse, a serpentine head suddenly filled his vision. Dark, jagged teeth gleamed in the light of his headlamp.

Maddock immediately changed directions. He drew his knife and slashed at the creature, and felt his blade strike something solid—harder than flesh.

He froze, his heart pounding double-time, and took a long look at the monster's head that loomed before him.

It was a carving about the size of a football. Silt and peat clung to it, obscuring the eyes and nostrils, but the toothy jaws shone in the lamplight. He reached out, still a little creeped out, and brushed it clean.

The years had robbed it of some of its fine detail, but it was still a remarkable piece. What was it doing down here? It hadn't simply been tossed into the water. Instead, it was affixed to a sheer rock wall a good twenty meters below the surface. It had to have been put here for a reason.

He took hold of it and pulled.

Nothing.

He tried again. Same result. He considered the problem for a few seconds.

Maybe it's a doorknob.

He tried turning it clockwise, but it held fast. One possibility remained. This time he turned it to the left.

Little by little, it moved a quarter turn and then stuck. Maddock heard a dull clacking sound, but nothing happened. He tried again to turn the sea serpent's head, but it wouldn't budge. It was time to get some added muscle.

He swam out of the crevasse, got Bones' attention, and guided him back to the serpent head. He made a quick rotating motion with his hands to show his friend what he had in mind. They set to work and this time, the serpent's head turned a full circle. Gears ground somewhere in the darkness, and then the rock wall before them slowly swung backward, revealing a wide, natural passageway running straight back in the direction of the castle. Wide enough, Maddock thought, for a prehistoric sea creature to swim through.

As usual, Bones didn't hesitate. He surged ahead like a torpedo, leaving Maddock to play catch-up.

It would serve you right if I held back and let the monster make you his midnight snack, Maddock thought. Then again, Bones would probably be an entree, and Maddock the main course.

The channel ran about fifty meters straight back, terminating in a large underground cavern. Maddock and Bones broke the surface to see two stone doors, each as large as the one through which they'd passed minutes before, standing open. They climbed out of the water and moved in for a closer look. The air was dank but breathable.

Rusted iron bars, as thick as Maddock's wrist, ran vertically through a broad slit in the door on the left. Broken chains lay strewn about, rust pitting the black links.

"Look at the bar on this thing." He pointed to the thick metal shaft, held in place by iron bands. "You slide that sucker into the wall and that door's not coming open easily."

"It was definitely built to keep something in," Maddock said.

Bones grimaced. "Like there's any doubt what that was."

Cautiously, they peered inside to see another large

cavern, this one with a deep pool in the middle. At the far end lay a huge, recessed overhang, the floor worn smooth. The remains of fish, seals, and a few humans lay scattered about.

"I think we've found the curse," Maddock said, "and it wasn't a virus."

"Looks like it's been empty for a long time," Bones said. "Doesn't bode well for the legend of the treasure, does it?"

"Let's take a look and see."

The second door was a solid block. It had no bar on the front—only a large keyed lock. The space beyond it was small, scarcely large enough for Maddock and Bones to stand side by side. Shelves carved from the bedrock lined the walls. All were bare.

"I don't see any sign of the Tuatha," Bones said. "No symbols, nothing."

"And these shelves weren't made for a sword or spear," Maddock agreed. "Maybe the stone or cauldron, if they're small enough, but I'm with you. I don't think it's Tuatha."

"But still, monsters and treasure," Bones said.

"Neither of which are here anymore. So unless you have an idea of what happened to them…" Maddock lapsed into silence as his eyes fell on a series of carvings on the back of the vault door. "What the hell are these?"

He and Bones shone their light on a pyramidal shape—but this pyramid was not formed from blocks.

"Are those severed heads?" Bones asked.

"Seven of them. I wonder what that means."

CHAPTER 25

Loch Ness

Isla's heart leaped when she peered out the window and saw Maddock and Bones coming down the road. She wanted to run down and meet them, but something told her to keep private things private. Even at this late hour, no telling who might be listening. She couldn't wait to see the look on Maddock's face when she told him what she'd found.

The soft knock came a minute later, and she opened the door to see the two treasure hunters, their hair still damp from the swim, standing in the hallway.

"We saw your light on," Maddock whispered. "Is it all right if we come in?"

"It's not that late," she said, then glanced at her bedside clock. One o'clock in the morning. "Well, it's not that late where you're from." She opened the door to let the two men in. "You can sit if you like."

Bones shook his head. "We've got wetsuits on under our clothes. I hope the chick at the front desk didn't think I'd wet my pants."

"She looked half-asleep to me," Maddock said, then turned to Isla. "Did you get the message off to Meikle?"

"I did. I believe I managed to make a fairly convincing forgery." At least, she hoped she'd succeeded.

"Think he bought it?"

She nodded. "He said he'd look into it right away. He didn't sound as if he suspected anything."

"Hopefully, that's the Tuatha off our tails for a while," Bones said.

"How was your dive?" she asked.

She listened, eyes wide, as the two men recounted their discovery of the sea serpent carving, the hidden door, and the chambers far beneath Urquhart Castle.

"Incredible. So there was some truth to the legend after all?"

Maddock nodded. "Except there was no pestilence. Only a monster, or monsters. At least, that's the way it looked to us."

"That's fascinating," she said.

"Problem is, it doesn't bring us any closer to the Tuatha treasure," Bones said. "Unless a bunch of severed heads are a clue."

The words jolted Isla all the way down to her toes. She blinked in surprise. "What did you say?"

"Severed heads. The treasure vault was empty, but someone carved seven heads on the inside of the door. We don't know for sure if it means anything, but as graffiti goes, it's kind of weird."

"And you're certain there were seven heads?" Her heart raced as she hurried to the desk and turned on her computer.

"What's going on?" Maddock said.

"There was a problem with a couple of the photographs you sent to Jimmy. The flash obscured some of the symbols."

"I told you, Maddock," Bones said. "You need to take that photography class with me."

"Taking photos of nude women for your friend's adult website is not a photography class. It's just creepy."

"I'd say getting engaged turned you into a bore, but you were always a dud," Bones replied.

Isla felt a pang of jealousy when she heard the word "engaged." *Grow up,* she told herself. *You barely know the man.* She opened the file containing the photographs Maddock had taken beneath Dunstaffnage, and showed them the obscured areas. Then she navigated to the photos Grizzly had taken.

Bones let out a low whistle. "Whoa! We missed some symbols."

"That's why the Well of the Dead clue was a bust," Maddock said. "Good thing Grizzly took some backup photos."

Isla smirked. "As much as I hate to say it, he does occasionally do something right. Though it's usually by accident."

"Were you able to decode the actual message?" Maddock asked.

Isla nodded. "The latter part of the message, the bit about St. Columba's beastie guarding the treasure, is the same, of course."

Bones folded his arms and arched his eyebrows. "All right, chick, don't keep us in suspense. Where is it?"

"Beneath the Well of the Seven Heads. I emailed your friend, Jimmy to show him what I found. He agrees with my translation. He also says you owe him an extra bottle of Wild Turkey for, and I quote, 'wasting his time with your crappy photography.'"

Maddock winced. "We do tend to dump on him a lot."

"*You* do," Bones said. "I like to solve my own problems."

"Only because you create so many of them for yourself." Maddock turned back to Isla. "Do you know where this Well of the Seven Heads is?"

"I do. And it's not far from here." She called up a map and showed them the location.

"Good," Maddock said. "I'm tempted to go there right now, but I'm exhausted. None of us will be at our best until we've had at least a few hours' sleep."

Bones nodded. "Up and out at 0500?"

"Works for me." Maddock turned to Isla. "Great work. We'll see you bright and early." He and Bones turned to leave.

Heart racing, Isla took a deep breath. "Maddock? Can you stay for a moment? I need to talk to you."

He and Bones both stopped and turned toward her.

"Just you," she said.

Bones looked like he was about to protest, but then Maddock gave a quick nod and made a small motion with his hand.

Bones gave Isla a long, hard look, then turned to Maddock. "I'll see you back in the room in a few minutes." He emphasized the last two words. When he left, he didn't close the door behind him.

"What's up?" Maddock asked, his expression unreadable.

"You asked about my parents. I thought I should answer your question."

He glanced at his watch. "Does it have to be right now?"

"Just listen. I trust you more than the others." She hurried to the door, glanced out into the hall to make certain Bones was not around, and then closed it behind her. How much to tell him?

"My parents weren't just obsessed with the Tuatha. They were members, and they were in deep."

Maddock frowned. "What, exactly, does that mean? What were they into?"

"They managed to hide almost everything from me. What I did learn, I picked up by snooping, eavesdropping. I can tell you that the Tuatha isn't all bad."

"Except when they're shooting at us or trying to kidnap you."

"I'm just saying their overall aims aren't the worst. They care about our history, our cultural heritage. They strive for unity instead of fragmentation. There's much in the past that binds the Irish, Scottish, and even some English and French together."

"That can be a good thing, or it can be a slippery slope toward xenophobia."

Isla shook her head. "I'm not making a lot of sense here. Bear with me." She took a deep breath. "For argument's sake, let's presume that there are," she paused, searching for the proper word, "powers that defy the laws of science."

Maddock nodded. "Go on."

"Let's also assume that at least some of the ancient legends are much more than that."

"I wouldn't be here if I didn't believe that." A strange glimmer sparkled in his blue eyes as he spoke. "It's one of those things I haven't told you about. I didn't want you to think Bones and I are crazy."

The tension drained from Isla's body, and she smiled. "Thank the gods. I've been holding this back, too. I believe the gods of the Tuatha are real, or at least, they were. I don't know if the treasures actually have any supernatural powers, but I'm open to the possibility. The Roman Empire and the Catholic Church shattered us. We lost our identity. Finding these treasures could bring back who we were."

Maddock took a step back, held up his hands. "I hear you, I really do. But I need you to understand. On more occasions than I can count, Bones and I have run up against people who had the same, exact idea, and none of them were what I would call good guys."

"It's not about that. It's about bringing back pride and hope, getting out from beneath the weight of oppression. I promise."

"How can you know that for certain if you aren't a part of the organization?"

Isla hung her head. "I suppose I can't, but I know my parents. Or at least, I knew them. They were decent people, and they wouldn't have supported a sinister agenda." A solitary tear traced a path down her cheek. She'd tried so hard not to think about her parents.

Maddock moved closer to her, so close they were almost touching.

"What happened to them?" he asked softly.

"They died a few years ago, while I was living in America. At least, that's what Fairly told me. They went to Patagonia in search of some lost Celtic tribe or some such. He said they died along with several other Tuatha in a massive cave collapse. Their bodies were never recovered."

"I'm sorry."

She felt Maddock's strong arms wrap around her, felt his tight embrace. And then he stepped back. "I'd better get back before Bones comes knocking on the door. Thanks for trusting me with this."

"Wait." Before she could change her mind, Isla

grabbed him around the neck and kissed him. For a brief, beautiful moment, she felt him respond. His hand moved to her shoulders.

And then, gently, he pushed her away.

"I'm sorry. I can't right now. I've got…"

"A fiancée." The bitterness of rejection tinged her words. "I understand."

"Exactly." He couldn't quite meet her eye as he spoke. "I'll see you in the morning."

He stepped out the door and gently closed it behind him, leaving Isla simmering in a stew of her own disappointment, jealousy, and anger.

The loud rumble of tires on gravel told Brown he'd once again drifted off the road. He was in desperate need of sleep, but after losing Isla Mulheron and her crew, his neck was on the chopping block. Literally. Brigid had told him as much when Brown had reported the tires being slashed on both of their vehicles.

There had been no dressing down from the leader of the Tuatha de Dannan. Not even a disapproving stare. Brigid simply made a call and had the tires replaced. Afterward, she handed the keys to Brown and said, "If you have not found Isla by the time I see you next, I will cut off your head."

The cold, matter of fact way in which she made the promise was the most chilling thing Brown had ever heard. In fact, the memory brought some life back to his fatigue-soaked brain.

He'd driven everywhere searching for any sign of Mulheron or the big American Indian with whom she appeared to be working. He'd searched all over Culloden, in case she'd tried to fool him by staying put. Then he drove around Inverness, checking hotel parking lots for a vehicle that resembled hers. The problem was, there were a fair number of red Kia Sportages in the city, all of which he had to check out, but none of those he saw bore the *Scottish Adventure* window sticker he was searching for. Finally, half on a hunch, half out of desperation, he'd driven to Loch Ness. It seemed like the sort of place the Tuatha would hide their treasure, though Brigid and Fairly insisted otherwise.

He'd circled the Loch half a dozen times, but still no sign of his quarry. He had to find her.

"Hells bells. What am I going to do?" he whispered. "I can't go back." Not for the first time tonight, he wondered what would happen if he just fled the country. Would Brigid bother to send someone after him? After all, the woman had said, "When I see you next." Maybe if she never saw Brown again…

The blare of a car horn brought him back to full alert. He had drifted into the oncoming lane! He yanked the wheel hard to the left to avoid an oncoming SUV. He jerked his head around to see a man giving him the finger. He couldn't believe it. It was the Indian!

His spirits buoyed, he watched in his rear-view mirror until the vehicle rounded a bend out of sight, then he made a quick U-turn. He'd follow them and try to avoid notice, but he was not going to let them out of his sight this time.

Should he report in now? Call for backup? Had he completed his task by finding Isla, or was the order to eliminate her companions still in play? He hadn't had the courage to ask. He mulled it over. Reaching out to Brigid was out of the question. The woman had hung a sword of Damocles over Brown's head, and she was a notoriously impatient type.

He'd take his chances with Fairly. He dialed the number and waited, heart in his throat, as it rang five, six, seven times before a tired voice answered.

"You're up early."

"Sorry," Brown said, "but I found Isa Mulheron, and I thought I should report in."

"And you didn't want to tell Brigid?"

"I got the impression she didn't want to hear from me until I'd finished the job. And I'm not sure if that job still includes killing Isla's traveling companions. Still, I thought her whereabouts shouldn't be kept a secret."

"Where is she?"

"Leaving Loch Ness. Heading south in a hurry."

Fairly fell silent for a moment. "Heading south. Must be on her way to Borthwick. But how did she know? Damn that Meikle. He's playing both sides."

"Borthwick?" Brown asked.

"Isla found a clue at Culloden. Meikle decoded it, says it points to Borthwick Castle."

Brown considered this new bit of information. It didn't sit well with him. He was certain Mulheron and her party had arrived at Culloden after the Tuatha, and had turned around and left right away.

"I think it's a red herring," he said.

"I've considered that possibility myself," Fairly said. "Follow them. Keep me apprised of their whereabouts."

"Brigid wanted them killed. At least, she wanted Isla's companions killed. Are those still my orders?"

The line went silent. After a few confused seconds in which Brown worried he'd dropped the call, Fairly cleared his throat.

"No. At least, not for the moment. Let Isla be our hound, sniffing out the treasure. It might be that her companions are providing essential support. I've kept an eye on her for years, and she made little progress until she joined forces with these men. Let's see what they accomplish. We can kill as many of them as we like when the time comes, assuming, of course, Brigid doesn't change her mind."

Brown nodded, though he knew Fairly couldn't see him. "You think she might decide to kill all of them?"

"Who can say? It's possible." Fairly cleared his throat. "And one more thing."

"What's that?" Brown asked.

"Whatever you do, don't lose them this time."

CHAPTER 26

Well of the Seven Heads, Invergarry

The sun was just peeking over the hills when they arrived at the Well of the Seven Heads. The monument stood on the shore of Loch Oich, south of Invergarry, and only a short drive from Loch Ness. One of the three lochs that comprised Scotland's Caledonian Canal, Oich was beautiful. Rolling hills and picturesque forests surrounded it on all sides. Maddock breathed in the crisp morning air as he took in the sights.

"This is weird," Bones said as they approached the monument. "I expected something, I don't know, older."

Maddock nodded. After the crumbled ruins of the castles they'd visited, the monument, set on a terrace overlooking the lake, with an ornate wrought-iron fence setting it apart, had a modern feel to it. It stood opposite a small shop, from which the pleasant aromas of coffee and baked goods wafted past them.

"Build it out of marble, and this thing wouldn't be out of place in Washington DC," Grizzly observed, gazing up at the dark stone memorial.

"It might be a bit grotesque for the National Mall," Maddock said.

Standing on a rectangular base, the black obelisk was topped by seven severed heads beneath a hand clutching a dagger. An inscription in an unfamiliar language covered panels on the sides.

"What language is this?" Grizzly asked.

"Gaelic. It tells the story behind the monument," Isla said.

"If it involves a bunch of severed heads, that's a story I definitely want to hear," said Bones.

"In 1663, two members of the MacDonnell clan were killed by their uncle and cousins in a brawl at a family mansion."

"Must have been some brawl," Maddock said.

"The young men had just returned from schooling in France, and their cousins started mocking their French accents and mannerisms."

"Okay, in that case, I'm on the cousins' side," Bones said.

Isla rolled her eyes. "Some say that was the reason, but others claim it was a setup. The killers, Alexander MacDonnell and his sons, were involved in a land dispute with the victims' side of the family. Resentment had been brewing for a while. In any case, justice was never served, which was typical for Scotland at a time when the clans wielded the real power."

"So who chopped their heads off?" Grizzly asked.

"The Poet Laureate."

Maddock couldn't help but laugh. "Seriously?"

"Iain Lom, known as Bald Iain, was the Gaelic Poet Laureate of Scotland, and a kinsman of the victims. He eventually decided to mete out justice himself. He set out on a crusade to make Alexander's branch of the MacDonnell family pay for what they'd done. Using his skills as an orator, and lots of biblical allusions, he rallied men to his cause and led them to the MacDonnell home at Inverlair, where the seven known killers were decapitated. They probably killed a lot more than that before it was over, but it was the seven killers the bard was after. He wrapped up the murderer's seven heads and took them to Invergarry Castle to present them to the father of the slain young men. On the way, he stopped here to wash the heads in the well and make them presentable. The site became notorious, and eventually, a monument was erected in 1812 by the chief of the MacDonnell Clan."

"It really exemplifies the time period," Maddock said. "It was the Wild West, Hatfields and McCoys."

"Save it, history nerd," Bones said. "You're boring the lady."

"Actually, I agree with him."

Isla glanced in Maddock's direction. They hadn't spoken about the previous night. Maddock searched her eyes for some indication of what she was feeling, but her gaze betrayed no emotion.

"I couldn't find a record of any monster sightings around here," Grizzly said, "but considering its proximity to Loch Ness, if we're accepting the theory that large, underwater channels lead to the sea, then it's not unreasonable to think some could also lead here."

Bones hopped the fence and circled the monument so he could examine it up close. After about ten seconds, he gave the stone obelisk a tentative shove. Then he pushed it harder.

Isla took a step forward, but Maddock pulled her back, gave a shake of his head, and held a finger to his lips.

Comprehension dawning in her eyes, she covered her mouth to stifle a laugh. Grizzly looked at them, frowning, but kept his silence. They watched as Bones wrapped his arms around the monument, grunted, and strained, trying to rotate it first to the right, then to the left. When Maddock could no longer watch him struggle, he cleared his throat.

"What are you doing there, big guy?"

Bones turned, wiped the sweat from his brow, and scowled at Maddock.

"What the hell does it look like I'm doing? I'm trying to find a secret door beneath the well. It would go faster if you'd help me, you know."

"Yeah, I get that," Maddock said, scratching his chin. "But why are you looking there?"

"What do you mean?"

"This is not the well; it's just a memorial. The well is down those stairs over there." He pointed to the left, where a set of steps wound down to the bottom of the terrace. A wooden sign reading *TO THE WELL* dangled from the metal railing.

Isla burst out laughing; Grizzly joined in a moment later.

Bones stood, hands on hips, glaring at each of them in turn. Finally, he gave his head a shake.

"Screw you guys. Every one of you."

Stepping over the rail, he descended the stairs, laughter following him down.

From the shelter of the trees, Brown watched as Isla Mulheron and her three companions examined the monument at the Well of Severed Heads, or whatever it was called. He wished he could hear what they were saying, but there was little cover between them and his hiding place. He watched as the big Indian examined the monument with care.

It was a grisly thing. The big hand, clutching a knife, appeared to be carrying the heads. That was Scotland at the time of the clans—a place where the strong survived. Brown let out a small, rueful laugh. He could trace his lineage back through many generations of Scots, yet here he was answering to Brigid, whose ancestors weren't even Scottish. The bloody Tuatha leader always favored the Irish. It would serve them right if the Scottish faction of the organization got hold of the treasure. After all, the stone, at least, was theirs by right, wasn't it?

He watched as his quarry descended the steps below the monument and disappeared. He waited, but they didn't come back up. Was there something down there, or were they exploring the lake shore? He'd have to move closer. Fairly had ordered him not to lose them again. Brown was already on the wrong side of Brigid. He didn't need to anger Fairly, too.

He decided to make a quick phone call first to let his superiors know that it looked like their mole had given them the wrong information. That ought to be a point in his favor, shouldn't it? Suddenly, Brown's information was more valuable than Meikle's. Smiling, he punched up Fairly's number.

"I've tracked them down to Invergarry, to Loch Loich," he said. "The Well of the Severed Heads."

"You mean the Well of the *Seven* Heads." Fairly spoke loudly, apparently for the benefit of whoever he was with.

"Damn that Meikle," a voice said in the background. It sounded like Brigid.

"What are they doing right now?" Fairly asked.

"They looked at the statue for a while, and then they went down a hill toward the lake. I'm about to follow them."

"There's no need," Fairly said. "I've been there before. The well lies underground beneath the statue. That's where they are going. We're not far from you, and can be there shortly." He paused. "Brigid wants to speak with you."

Brown's stomach lurched as Brigid's voice filled his ear.

"Brown, I want you to listen carefully. Keep an eye on the entrance to the well. Let us know if Isla and her party come out again. Do not go down into the well yourself. I don't want you making a botch of this. Understood?"

Brown struggled to keep his anger in check. "Yes," he said, his voice flat.

"Good." Brigid ended the call.

Brown stared at his cell phone screen for three angry seconds before cursing and shoving it into his pocket. He was fed up with Brigid. How much longer would he kowtow to the woman? He ought to follow Isla into the well, and if the treasure was there, he'd take it for himself. No, he could take it for Scotland. He hesitated. This was foolish talk. There were four of them and only one of him. And even if he succeeded, he'd be crossing not only Brigid but all of the Tuatha de Dannan. Sighing, he put his phone back into his pocket and waited.

CHAPTER 27

The Well of the Seven Heads, Invergarry

An arched doorway opened onto the dark tunnel that led to the well beneath the seven heads monument. Beneath his feet, the weathered, chipped stonework showed signs of great age. Patches of weeds grew from the cracks as far back as the sunlight could reach, lending a splash of color to the uniform gray. Moisture oozed down from above, staining the rocks. Maddock ran his hand along the rough, gray stone, cold at his touch. His fingertips brushed over green patches of thin, mossy growth.

"It feels like the entrance to an old dungeon," Grizzly said.

"Let's just hope no one locks us in," Isla replied.

The passage came to a dead end, the scant light revealing only a few of its secrets. Maddock and Bones flicked on their Maglites and shone them all around. Another, lower archway marked the end of the passage, and just beyond it lay the Well of the Seven Heads.

"Not very big," Bones said.

Maddock shook his head. "Nor very deep."

He knelt for a closer look. In the crystal clear water, he could see the bottom of the well, several feet beneath the surface. Unlike the rough stone of the tunnel in which they stood, the stonework at the bottom of the well was precise, each stone fitted neatly together.

"The clue does say 'under' the well," Maddock said. "And I've got a feeling that bottom was added to hide whatever is down there."

"Okay, who wants to be the one to test your theory?" Bones said.

"Worried about shrinkage again?" Maddock asked.

Isla covered her mouth to stifle a giggle. Bones rolled his eyes but didn't reply.

"I'll do it." Maddock handed his phone, wallet,

pistol, and flashlight to his partner. "Give me some light down there, all right?" Before he could change his mind, he braced himself, took a couple of breaths, and plunged feet first into the well.

The sudden immersion was a shock to his system. His thoughts immediately flashed to a fall into icy water off the coast of Wrangel Island, years ago. *Okay, it isn't that bad,* he thought. He forced his eyes open, waited a few seconds to adjust to the stinging, chilly water, and looked around.

Rough stonework lined the sides of the well, except for the row at the bottom. These stones were regular in shape, finely honed. He searched them one by one, and his eyes fell on a familiar symbol—the cauldron. Excited, he turned quickly and found at the compass points the remaining symbols—sword, spear, and stone. It was just like the chamber beneath Dunstaffnage.

He gave each stone a careful inspection, poking and prodding them one by one, pushing and pulling, trying to release a hidden latch. Nothing. Lungs burning, he went up for a breath of air.

"How we doing down there?" Bones asked.

The frigid water of the well seemed to have deprived Maddock of speech, so he shook his head numbly and went back down.

The stones were obviously a dead end. There must be something he was missing. He repositioned himself and examined the floor. After several seconds, he spotted what he had previously overlooked. Faint lines ran across the floor. He moved higher until he could take it in—the face of the Celtic goddess Danu! Her image was rendered in shallow cuts, easy to overlook. Furthermore, if viewed from too close up, it would look like random lines running across the stone. He was certain it meant something, but what?

He stared down at the face, his eyes burning from the cold water. Invisible bands seemed to constrict his chest. He'd need more air soon.

And then he spotted it. Danu's open mouth was

formed from rock a shade darker than the rest. He swam down for a closer look and saw that its edges rose a few millimeters above the surrounding floor. Was it a plug?

He tried to take hold of it, but his numb fingers cold not grip the scant edge. Next, he took out his knife and tried to work the plug out with its sharp point. No joy.

His body now screamed for air. Spots appeared in front of his eyes. He needed to go up again, but stubbornness held him in place.

Damn! There's got to be a way.

Anger surging through him, he rose, braced himself against the sides of the well, and stamped down hard with the heel of his booted foot.

Nothing.

He stamped again, and this time he thought he heard a dull, crackling sound. Again and again, he hammered his foot against the stone plug until finally, it shattered.

And then, with alarming suddenness, the floor fell away beneath his feet. He had only a moment to wonder what he had done before a loud, sucking sound filled his ears, and he was swept down into darkness.

"He needs to hurry up," Bones said, shining his light down into the well. He couldn't tell what exactly Maddock was doing, but it was clearly ineffectual. "I need coffee, and we might have to form a new plan."

"This has to be it," Isla said. "There's only one Well of the Seven Heads. The clue at Dunstaffnage, the carving at Urquhart, everything points here."

"I get it, but unless he finds something…" He paused. His sharp ears picked up a dull, thumping sound, like someone hammering from a great distance away. And then a crackling sound that grew louder. Instinctively he looked up, fearing that the ceiling were about to come down.

"The water!" Isla shouted. "What's happening?"

The surface of the well roiled. A vortex formed at the center, spinning into a whirlpool as the water drained away in a rush. Bones turned his light down into the well and found only a deep hole.

Maddock was gone.

"Maddock!" Bones shouted.

"Oh my God! What's happened to him?" Isla clutched Bones' arm. "We have to get down there now. What if he's hurt? What if he's…" She couldn't finish the sentence. Tears welled in her eyes.

"I'm sure he's okay," Grizzly said. "We had a nice little fall when I found the trapdoor at Dunstaffnage, and we came out of it all right."

Isla nodded and scrubbed at her face with the back of her sleeve. "Sorry for my reaction. I'm exhausted and have been on edge for days."

Bones wasn't sure he bought her explanation, but he let it go.

"Want me to go down and look for him?" Grizzly asked.

"Yeah, headfirst," Bones said.

Grizzly tilted his head, a slight frown creasing his brow. Then he laughed. "You always trip me up with your sense of humor."

"I imagine a lot of things trip you up." Bones still couldn't quite believe that the cryptid hunter whom he'd so admired had turned out to be such a disappointment. Sure, the guy knew his monsters, but in every other area, he was woefully lacking. With a wry shake of his head, he turned his attention to Isla. "You going to be all right?"

"I think so. But if something happens to Maddock, I don't know what I'll do."

Suspicion flared inside him. Had things between her and Maddock gone farther than he'd thought? Surely not. Maddock had returned from her room after only a few minutes the night before. No time for anything serious to happen.

"Chick, you hardly know him."

"I just meant because I got you two into this," she said much too quickly.

"Relax, we're free agents. When it comes to our work, that is." He cast a meaningful glance at her, and she lowered her head.

"I think we can get down there," he said, shining his light down the well. "It only drops a couple of feet below where the floor was, and then it looks like it angles out. Might be like a water slide going down, which could be dangerous. Maybe you two should wait here while I check it out."

Isla gave a firm shake of her head. "I'm going too."

"Me, too," Grizzly added. "The treasure is down there, and maybe the monster. That's where I need to be."

"Great," Bones said. "Just stay behind me and try not to slip. If you come crashing down on top of me, I'll be highly pissed."

A dark sense of foreboding creeping over him, Bones lowered himself into the well.

CHAPTER 28

Beneath the Well of the Seven Heads

Maddock careened down the steep passageway. He grabbed for a handhold, tried to use his feet to slow his fall, but he could find no purchase on the water and grime-slicked stone surface. Worn smooth by the passage of water and time, the channel down which he slid was like a tube. He slid along the slimy rock, oddly unaware of how fast he was moving in the pitch darkness. *Bones would think this was a blast,* he thought.

And then he hit level ground. It happened so suddenly he scarcely had time to protect his head before he was tumbling across a rough stone floor. His body found every bump in the uneven surface, and then he crashed into a solid wall. Sparks flashed as his head struck rock, and hot pain coursed through him.

"I don't even have Grizzly to blame for this," he muttered to no one.

He lay there, flat on his back, arms and legs splayed out, breathing heavily. He concentrated on listening to the messages his body was sending him. Which parts were injured and how badly? He'd wrenched his back, but he thought his spine was uninjured. He checked it by wiggling his fingers and toes. At least, it felt like they wiggled; he couldn't see an inch in front of his face in the pitch black. Next, he flexed his arms and legs. Everything seemed okay there as well. After a quick head-to-toe assessment, he diagnosed himself with a bump on the head, a few bruised ribs, and a similarly injured kneecap.

Satisfied that he was going to live, he decided it was time for action. His hand found the wall next to him, and he rose to his feet. A wave of dizziness washed over him, but he managed to remain standing. Maybe the blow to the head was worse than he thought. He sucked in a few deep breaths and waited for the dizzy spell to pass.

"Okay," he said, "no light, and no idea what's down here. I guess I can find the tunnel and try to crawl back up, or I can wait and see if Bones and the others come down."

The decision was taken out of his hands when he heard Bones' voice echo through the chamber.

"Hooooly craaaap!" Bones rumbled. And then, "Everybody make yourselves into a ball!"

"Wish I'd thought of that," Maddock muttered.

And then he heard a soft thumping sound and his feet flew out from under him as something, rather someone, crashed hard into his legs. He hit the ground hard, the wind forced out of him, as new spears of pain lanced through his side. And then, one after another, two more bodies crashed into him.

"Seriously?" he gasped. "Not one of you managed to avoid hitting me?"

"Maddock? Are you all right?" He felt Isla's hand on his cheek, her breath damp on his neck. As if of its own volition, one of his hands found hers and gave it a squeeze, but she jerked it away. "Just checking," she snapped.

Still angry about last night, I suppose.

And then a light blossomed in the darkness.

"That was actually kind of fun," Bones said. "Except for the part where Maddock kicked me in the head."

"Kicked you?" Maddock said, still regaining his breath. "You three treated me like a bowling pin."

"Yeah, but I'm the one who managed to pick up the spare. Can you stand?"

Maddock nodded and allowed his friend to haul him to his feet. Everything hurt. Bones returned Maddock's belongings to him, and Maddock added his own light to the one Bones held. A moment later, Isla and Grizzly clicked on their flashlights. After the pitch black, the cavern now seemed bright as day.

It was a domed chamber, maybe thirty feet across. Up ahead, a wide opening led into a dark passageway beyond. And all around the entryway lay…

"Skeletons!" Isla gasped.

Human bones lay scattered across the floor. The beam of Maddock's light fell upon a skull; its open mouth and empty eye sockets appeared to gape at him, as if shocked by this intrusion into its final resting place. Here and there he saw bits of leather and fabric, metal buttons, and rusted weapons.

"Who were they?" Grizzly asked.

"And who killed them?" Isla added.

Maddock moved closer to examine one of the skeletons that remained mostly intact.

"I don't think it's a question of who," he said, "but what. Look at this guy."

The others moved in around him for a closer look.

"His left foot is gone like it was bitten clean off. Same with his right hand."

"Why do you say 'bitten'?" Isla whispered.

"It's too clean. If either were hacked off with, say, a sword, or blown off by a gunshot, you'd see shattered bone, fragmentation, crushing."

Grizzly swallowed hard, let out an audible gulp. "Couldn't a sword slice through cleanly?"

"The right sword, wielded by the right man, striking the right place, maybe. But look how high up on the leg it's severed. See the thickness of the bone? Something powerful sliced through this man's leg like it was nothing."

"Hold on," Grizzly said. "I can't believe that Nessie is a killing machine. I just can't. There's no record of her attacking anyone."

"Except the German soldiers on the U-boat," Bones said.

"Remember the clue?" Isla prompted. "The beastie guards the treasure. Maybe when the monster's down here it's more...territorial?"

"It looks like these bodies have been down here a while," Maddock said. "It looks like this guy was wearing a tunic." He pointed first to the moldering remains of a loose-fitting, knee-length shirt clinging to the skeleton, and then to the claymore, its blade pitted with rust, lying nearby. "But the well, and the false bottom were built long after these guys died."

"So the Tuatha chose a cavern where the beastie lives as the place to hide their treasure," Bones said. "Makes sense."

"It would definitely present a challenge to the unworthy," Isla added.

"Maybe there's no monster. Perhaps they just put these skeletons here to scare us off," Grizzly said.

"If you don't want to go on, you don't have to," Maddock told the cryptid hunter. "But I'm not stopping."

Grizzly held up his hands. "Nobody said anything about stopping. It's just, you two have guns, and I don't want you getting trigger-happy if we encounter an unknown creature. Just," he looked up, searching for the words, "give her a chance."

Maddock nodded. "Fair enough. We don't use deadly force unless it's in defense of our lives." He turned and shone his beam down the dark passageway. "Now, let's see what's back there."

Brigid descended the steps, the cool breeze off of Loch Oich ruffling her auburn hair. She looked out at the water and sighed. She wanted to believe this was it—that they were finally on the verge of discovery. But there had been so many disappointments, so many bumps in the road. And then there had been the impediments. They would have to be removed post-haste.

She sighed. Isla could present a problem. She was as dedicated to the search for the treasure as Brigid was, but could Isla be made to see the big picture? If not, steps would have to be taken. The thought pained Brigid, but that was a problem that would sort itself out in time.

At the mouth of the passageway that led to the Well of the Seven Heads, she paused. The footsteps behind her stopped. In addition to Fairly and O'Brien, she'd brought extra muscle along in the form of Donovan, a former cop with a penchant for excess violence, and Donnelly, a big, bald woman whom she'd hired away from a musician's private security detail.

"What is it?" Fairly whispered.

Brigid held up a hand. Cautiously, she leaned forward and stole a glance down the tunnel. No one was there.

"Just checking." She looked around. "Where the hell has Brown gotten to?"

"I'm here." Brown stepped out from behind one of the many trees that ringed the Loch. "They went in right about the time I called you, and they haven't come out."

Brigid's heart raced. "So they must have found something!" Hope rose within her. She sensed that, at long last, they had reached the end of their quest. This time, they would find it. "Let's go."

She led the way down the tunnel, taking care to move soundlessly. No need to alert Isla should she be somewhere nearby. The passageway faded to black, and she took out a flashlight and flicked it on.

"That's the well?" O'Brien whispered from somewhere behind them. "But there's no water."

Brigid knelt and shone her light down into the gaping hole. "There was a false bottom, but someone has broken through. See?" She played her light around the well, several feet down. Jagged chunks of rock stuck out perpendicular from the wall.

"Isla," Fairly said.

Brigid nodded. "She's a clever one. Resourceful." Worry filled her as she spoke. Isla was a diligent researcher with a sharp mind and could be a valuable resource. Surely she could be brought around. But how much did Brigid really know about the young journalist? Perhaps Isla couldn't be trusted.

"When we catch up with them, what are our orders?" O'Brien asked.

"When we get down there, you are free to kill the men, but do not shoot Isla unless I give the order. She could still prove valuable."

"But, there's a chance you might want her dead?" Fairly asked. "That would be a shame."

"It would. She has been a faithful hound over the years even if she didn't know it. Her father's influence. He loved a treasure hunt."

"He surely did," Fairly agreed.

Brigid nodded. "She, and whoever these men are, have hopefully led us to the treasure. If she won't see reason, we will have to accept that her usefulness is at an end. We can't leave a single enemy alive to interfere with our plans moving forward."

Fairly nodded. "If I may make a suggestion, why follow them down into God knows what? Let them bring the treasure out, and we'll take it from them."

Brigid shook her head. "Too many things could go wrong. The Tuatha might have built in a back door, in which case they could find another way out. Or they could hide the treasure, intending to return for it later."

"I agree," Brown interrupted.

Brigid turned a withering gaze upon her underling, but the man did not flinch.

"This is the treasure of the Tuatha de Dannan," Brown continued. "A reward for the worthy. It is not for the fearful, who cower while others claim it. We should go down there and take it. For Scotland."

Brigid set her jaw and stared at Brown. This insubordination should not go unpunished, but Brown's words had had the desired effect. Where she had seen trepidation, even fear, moments before, she now saw determination in the faces of Fairly and O'Brien. He stood.

"Well spoken, Mister Brown. How about you lead the way down into the well?"

CHAPTER 29

Beneath the Well of the Seven Heads

Maddock played the beam of his Maglite all around as they moved down the wide, gently sloping tunnel. In the quiet, he could hear only their soft footfalls and the occasional dripping of water onto the floor. A chill ran down his neck. It was cold down here, their light clothing doing little to ward off the dampness.

Isla broke the silence. "There are cracks everywhere down here." She ran her finger across a split in the rock that oozed water. "That doesn't exactly fill me with confidence."

"It'll be all right," Bones said. "It's like a Hoover Dam tour."

"I have no idea what you're talking about."

Bones raised his voice a notch and gave it a nasal quality. "I'll be your dam guide. Feel free to take all the dam pictures you want."

Isla gave him a blank stare. "Still nothing."

"Are there any dam questions?" Bones continued.

Maddock chimed in. "Where can I get some damn bait?"

Grizzly put his arm around Isla's shoulders. "If you've got some chewing gum, I could try plugging some of those cracks for you."

The three men guffawed.

"Come on," Bones said. "*Vegas Vacation*? Chevy Chase? Cousin Eddie?"

"I hate you all." Isla turned around and stalked away down the passage.

"It's cool," Bones said. "When this is over we'll rent the movie. You'll love it."

His words were cut off by Isla's loud cry.

"Guys! Get in here now!"

Maddock hurried after her, following the glow of her light. He rounded a bend and skidded to a halt, the damp stone slick beneath his feet.

"What is it?" he asked.

Isla snaked an arm around his waist. Her breath coming in rapid gulps, she pointed a trembling finger.

They stood at the edge of a small underground lake, its dark surface smooth as glass. As Maddock's eyes ran across it, a single drop of water fell from the ceiling, partially concealed by a curtain of mist, and struck with a gentle *plink*. Ripples radiated out. The beam of his light followed them until they reached a rocky islet at the lake's center.

Bones and Grizzly caught up with them and stood gaping at what they saw.

It was not the small island itself that was remarkable, but what it held. The middle of the gray slab of stone was worn down in a deep, rounded indentation like a wallow, similar to what they'd seen below Urquhart Castle. How large a creature and how much time had it taken to wear down the stone like that? But that wasn't what captured Maddock's imagination.

In the middle of the wallow, lying amongst fish bones and other detritus lay the remains of a juvenile plesiosaur.

Even to Maddock's untrained eye, the skeleton was immediately recognizable. He'd seen enough fossils and images of its adult counterparts to know the distinctive long neck, serpentine head, and powerful flippers.

"It's a baby," Isla whispered.

"And it's not fossilized," Bones said. "There's still some tissue on the carcass." He trained the beam of his light on the skeletal remains of the tail, where a few bits of dark flesh clung stubbornly to bone.

"Do you think it's a nest?" Isla asked.

"I'm not sure," Grizzly said. "The current theory among scientists is the plesiosaur didn't lay eggs, but gave birth to live young, usually one at a time, and probably didn't spend much time on land. Maybe this little guy was sick and unable to swim?" The tone of genuine sympathy in the man's voice struck a chord with

Maddock. Grizzly might be a buffoon, but he had a heart.

"This is incredible!" Isla said, taking out her camera. "Even if we don't find the treasure, this alone could make my career."

"You know what this means, don't you, Maddock?" Bones said. "We just proved that plesiosaurs not only live in this area but have survived undetected."

Maddock nodded. This was the sort of thing he'd fantasized about as a kid, though he'd always wanted to see a live specimen. Now that he'd seen evidence of their ferocity, though, he wasn't so sure.

Isla and Grizzly spent a few minutes taking photographs, Grizzly vowing to return with a camera crew.

"Jo Slater is going to freak when she finds out. Hell, they might give me her show."

Bones turned a questioning look in his direction. "You know Slater?"

"Not really. She thinks she's too good for the likes of me." Grizzly frowned. "Do *you* know her?"

Bones coughed delicately, cleared his throat. "We've, um, hung out together."

"That means he hooked up with her and she never called again," Maddock explained.

"Hey, it's not like that," Bones said. "I mean, I didn't call her either. At least, not after..." He gave his head a shake. "Screw you, Maddock."

"When we release our findings," Grizzly said, "she'll be calling. And you and I can have the pleasure of telling her where to go." He sat down and began unlacing his boots.

"What are you doing?" Maddock asked.

"I'm going to swim out there and check it out up close." Grizzly inclined his head toward the islet.

"There will be time for that, later. Right now we're going to keep searching for the treasure. Besides," he paused for effect, "you never know. That thing's mother might be out there somewhere, and she's probably pissed."

Grizzly pursed his lips, looked out at the dark water, and nodded. "Good point. I'll wait."

"You should have let him go," Bones whispered, too soft for anyone but Maddock to hear.

A narrow shelf skirted the shore of the underground lake, and they followed it, careful not to slip. Maddock's words had put everyone on high alert. It seemed the legend was true; a beastie did guard whatever lay hidden down here. The skeletons in the first chamber gave mute witness to the danger posed by the creatures that dwelled here.

Maddock rested his hand on the pistol in his pocket. Eight bullets in the magazine. Bones was similarly armed. Were they crazy? If they did, in fact, encounter a hostile creature, would that be enough firepower to hold it at bay until they made their escape?

"Everybody hold on." He turned and held up a hand, stopping them in their tracks. "I just want to make sure everyone understands the danger."

"Here we go," Bones said, rolling his eyes. "Next he'll offer to wipe our butts for us."

"Look," Maddock said. "If we encounter one of these monsters, I can't guarantee we'll be able to fight it off. I'm willing to take the risk, and I'm sure Bones is too, but we're crazy like that. What about you two?"

"Cryptids are my life. I'm going on no matter what anyone else does," Grizzly said.

"And I feel the same about the treasure," Isla said. "It's in my blood. It's mine."

"All right. We'll go on." Maddock wasn't sure if he was relieved or not. He hadn't missed the way Isla said, "It's mine." Was she coming down with treasure fever? Had she had it all along, and he'd missed the signs? A lifelong pursuit such as hers could have profound effects on one's psyche. He'd have to keep an eye on her.

At the far end of the cavern, they moved into another passageway through which a deep channel flowed. Maddock shone his beam down into the water and saw movement, flashes of silver.

"Salmon," Grizzly said. "I guess we know what the creatures eat."

"Salmon and people who are stupid enough to get in their way," Bones said.

"If it comes to that, we're sacrificing you," Maddock said. "You've got the most meat on your bones. Pun intended."

Bones grinned. "Looks like I won't be the first. Check that out." He pointed out into the water.

Up ahead, the channel widened around another rocky islet. There, in the midst of fish and seal bones, a human skull grinned back at them.

"Looks like meat's back on the menu, boys," Isla said. After a long pause, she threw up her hands. "Oh, come on! *Lord of the Rings*?"

"We got the reference," Maddock said. "We're just surprised you knew it."

She rolled her eyes. "I know a little geek culture. The *Vacation* movies don't qualify."

"That's debatable," Bones said.

Isla turned to argue, but Maddock grabbed her by the arm.

"What is it?"

Slowly, he turned her around so she could see what he was looking at. Up ahead lay another underground lake. A series of stone steps led across the surface of the water to another islet. At the center stood the Goddess Danu, surrounded by four pedestals, and atop them…

Isla gasped. "The treasure!"

CHAPTER 30

The Shrine of Danu

A statue of the Goddess Danu, perfectly preserved, stood facing them. Several small chests lay broken at her feet, spilling gold and jewels. Carved into the stone floor, the swirling pattern of a Celtic triskele encircled her. At the edges of the islet stood four sturdy blocks of basalt, each supporting one of the treasures of the Tuatha de Dannan.

"It's just like the shrine underneath Dunstaffnage," Maddock said.

"Except this time, the treasure is actually here," Grizzly said. "The gold and jewels must be the Urquhart Treasure. Moved here for safe keeping, I suppose."

Isla took out her camera and began clicking away. "Go on," she said to Maddock and Bones. "I'll photograph you making your way out to the island. Just don't touch anything until I get there."

"Wouldn't dream of it," Maddock said. He paused to inspect the stepping stones that led out to the island shrine. Each was about one-foot square and jutted up just above the surface. They appeared solid, carved from the native stone of the cavern. But would they support his weight? Only one way to find out.

Gingerly, he stepped onto the first stone, testing it before putting his weight on it. It held. He took the next step with similar care.

"Any day now, Grandma," Bones said.

By the third stone, Maddock had gained enough confidence that he moved at a regular pace, counting them as he went. Ten, eleven, twelve... He froze.

"What is it?" Bones asked.

"The last stone is missing." Where the thirteenth stone should have been lay a stretch of open water.

"So jump," Grizzly suggested.

"You don't know Maddock," Bones said. "He'll stand

there for a half hour just to make sure everything's cool. Finally, he'll jump, and everything will be cool, but will he learn? Not a chance."

"Just playing it safe." Maddock gazed at the water, then up to the ceiling, far above, and finally to the shrine. He could see no sign of a booby trap or any other danger. Most likely there had once been a thirteenth stone, rigged to undercut the efforts of an unlucky treasure hunter. Hopefully whatever sort of trap it had been was like a mousetrap—once sprung, it was useless unless someone came along and reset it.

Might as well go for it. He tensed and sprang. He was no long jumper, but he cleared the water with ease, landing smoothly and turning to face the others.

"What are you waiting for, Bones? Not scared, are you?"

Bones laughed and, taking the stepping stones two at a time just to show off, made his way across to join Maddock. Grizzly followed, stopping periodically to turn toward Isla and smile for the camera. He didn't seem to notice that she stopped clicking the shutter every time he struck a pose.

"Clear the way," Grizzly warned as he reached the last stepping stone. "I don't want to knock you over."

Maddock looked down. He stood a good five feet from the water's edge. Unless the cryptid hunter grew wings, he wasn't covering that kind of distance. Still, he moved a few inches to the side just to humor the man.

"Isla, you might want to get this," Grizzly called. "Maybe get me in midair. That would make a great cover photo for your magazine."

Bones turned to Maddock. "Want me to push him in?"

Maddock laughed. "Nah. Let's keep him around. You never know when you might need a meat shield or a sacrificial lamb."

Grizzly tensed and sprang, legs splayed, one hand held high above his head.

"Michael Jordan!" Grizzly cried. His feet hit the

rocky island right at the edge of the water. For two comical seconds, he teetered on the edge, his arms windmilling wildly. And then, with a shout of, "Whoa!" he fell backward.

Quick as a mongoose, Bones reached out, snatched the man by his belt, and yanked him forward onto the island. He was rougher than absolutely necessary, and Grizzly ended up on his hands and knees at Bones' feet.

"Did you get that?" Bones called to Isla.

"You bet your ass I did!" she said, holding up her camera. "Probably not front-page material." She replaced her camera in its waterproof case, tucked it into her drawstring bag, and made her way across the steps. "This is not my idea of fun," she said as she leaped from one rock to the next. "They made us do hurdles in physical education. I've avoided jumping on principal ever since."

"Seriously?" Maddock asked as she landed on the last stepping stone.

"Not really," she said, laughing. "I'm just worried that I'll slip and get my camera wet. Speaking of my camera…" She slipped out of her drawstring bag. "Hold this, just in case." She tossed it underhand to Maddock. In doing so, she overbalanced. "Oh, bollocks!" She tried to jump but made it only a couple of feet before hitting the water.

"Isla!" Maddock shouted.

She surfaced a moment later, shuddering and spewing a stream of curses.

"Can you swim?" Grizzly asked.

"Of course I can swim, you bloody…" She halted in mid-sentence and gasped, her wide eyes staring at something off to the side.

"What is it?" Maddock asked, sweeping the beam of his light across the surface of the lake.

"Th…th…there. Coming this way."

And then Maddock saw it. Three dark humps sliced through the water, making a beeline for Isla.

Brigid shone her light across the dark water to the

small, stone islet. It took all her self-control to keep her features fixed as she gazed upon what was obviously the remains of an aquatic reptile. Odd, despite having believed the legends of the Tuatha de Dannan, having read the clue that said it was guarded by a beastie, she had never put any stock in Nessie lore. She'd always believe it a foolish local legend, repeated and embellished to encourage tourism. Furthermore, she'd assumed the Tuatha had capitalized on the tales in order to frighten the unworthy.

"It seems there was something to the legends after all," she said.

"You mean that thing is real?" O'Brien asked.

"No," Brigid said, derision strong in her voice. "Someone made a fake sea monster skeleton and hid it down here where no one would ever stumble across it, and then sealed up the well just to make certain."

"I only meant, perhaps it's a forgery intended to frighten anyone who comes looking for the treasure," O'Brien said dully.

"Lower your voices," Brigid said. "The others are somewhere up ahead. We don't want to alert them to our presence."

"They aren't the only ones I don't wish to alert," Fairly said delicately. "If this beastie has brothers and sisters about…"

"Then Isla and her men will encounter the beasts first," Brigid said. "Perhaps the guardian of the treasure will take care of them for us." Her guts knotted as she spoke. What if Isla fell victim to the beast?

"But if that happens, who will take care of the guardian?" Brown asked.

Standing a few paces away, Donnelly grinned and cracked her knuckles. "We will." She patted the pistol holstered at her hip.

Brigid nodded. There were six of them, all armed and ready. She hoped that would be enough.

CHAPTER 31

The Shrine of Danu

The line of dark humps undulated as it zipped silently through the water. As Bones and Grizzly hauled Isla up onto dry land, Maddock drew his pistol and took aim. Did he dare fire? Would a bullet only anger the beast? Could he say for certain that it meant them any harm?

"Everybody move to the center, next to the statue," he said.

"Is this a good idea?" Bones asked, taking up a position in front of the others. "If this thing guards the treasure, we're standing at ground zero."

"The other option is to run, but I don't relish hopping back across those stepping stones with that thing out there."

As they watched, the humps veered away from the island and began a slow, wide circle around the underground lake. When it seemed the thing would come no closer, they all relaxed, though Maddock kept his pistol in his hand.

"So it really does have humps," Grizzly marveled. "I guess it's to be expected that the plesiosaur would evolve some unique traits over time."

"How big do you think it is?" Isla asked.

Maddock gazed at the strange sight. Visions of all the alleged Loch Ness monster photos he'd seen over the years ran through his mind. "Difficult to say. The humps are barely breaking the water, but if they comprise the length of the body, then I guess triple it to account for the neck and tail."

"About six meters, or twenty feet. Not a large one, then," Isla said.

"Works for me," Bones said. "The shorter the neck, the less chance it has of reaching out and snatching one of us."

Maddock grimaced. "Unless it climbs up here with

us."

"Well, aren't you just a ray of sunshine?"

As if on cue, the line of humps turned and headed directly toward them. Once again, Maddock raised his pistol and took aim.

"Holy crap." Bones took out his own pistol and moved to stand beside his friend. "Do we wait to see the whites of its eyes?"

"I don't know. Just make your shots count."

The humps drew closer. Maddock placed his finger on the trigger.

Twenty feet. Ten feet.

And then something broke the water. A sleek, round, fur-covered head with a long snout and big, dark eyes.

Maddock huffed a laugh and sagged with relief as two more heads popped up. One let out a low, barking sound and rolled over.

"Seals," Isla said. "How did we not realize?"

"Too freaked out," Grizzly said.

"One of the theories behind the Loch Ness phenomenon is the rows of humps people have reported seeing are, in fact, seals. Supposedly, mammals tend to swim up and down, giving the appearance of humps, while serpents swim more side to side," Bones said. "I think that's a good sign—two SEALs show up and along come a bunch of seals."

Isla frowned and cocked her head. "You know, you're just as dumb below ground as you are up above."

"Give me time," Bones said. "I grow on you."

"Like a fungus," Maddock added.

"Now that we've been granted a reprieve," Isla began, "how about we examine the treasure?"

"Definitely." The tension of the previous moments had momentarily swept away the joy of discovery. Now, the thrill returned as he turned to gaze at the Treasure of the Tuatha de Dannan.

Atop the basalt block in which the word *Dagda* was carved stood a cauldron cast from a golden-bronze metal. A triskele was engraved inside it, framing a whiskey colored gem set in the bottom.

Isla snapped a couple of photographs, then lowered her camera and stared reverentially at the legendary object. "From Muirias was brought the cauldron of the Dagda. No company went away from it unsatisfied," she whispered. "That's what was written about it, anyway. But there was no mention of a gemstone."

"That's really weird," Grizzly said, reaching toward the cauldron.

Maddock grabbed his wrist. "Haven't we discussed touching things? As in, you don't do it."

Grizzly took a step back, fists clenched, jaw set. "I'm getting a little tired of this. Nobody put you in charge."

"I'm taking charge, and you can either accept that or do something about it. Decide now." He took a step toward the cryptid hunter.

Grizzly wilted beneath Maddock's cold stare. He held up his hands. "Calm down. I'm just saying you don't have to be an ass all the time."

"You know, Maddock, you really are an ass most of the time," Bones added.

"I'll work on my people skills when this is over." Maddock turned away from the cauldron and moved on to inspect the spear. The pedestal in which it was set was labeled *Lug*. A hole had been drilled in the top so that the spear could stand upright. The shaft was not made of wood, but appeared to be formed of the same shiny metal as the cauldron. As with the cauldron, wavy lines climbed the shaft like creeping vines, up to a triskele that wrapped around a blood red gem set just beneath the gleaming spear head.

"What was the story behind this one?" Bones asked Isla.

"From Goirias was brought the spear had by Lug," she recited. "No battle was sustained against it nor against the man who held it in his hand."

"That sounds like the legend associated with another spear," Bones said.

"The Spear of Destiny?" Grizzly said. "Do you think

this could be it?"

"Doubtful," Bones said. He glanced at Maddock, who gave a small shake of his head. This wasn't the time to recount their previous adventures, nor was Grizzly a trustworthy audience.

But Grizzly had already turned to examine the sword. "*Nuada*," he read from the face of the pedestal. "They ought to call it Excalibur, the way they've got it stuck into the stone."

Indeed, a slot had been cut into the surface of the rock and the sword of the Tuatha stood, point down in the rock. Like the other objects, it too was made of the strange, coppery-gold alloy. A stone of deep sapphire was set in the pommel, surrounded by the now-familiar triskele.

Isla snapped more photographs. "The sword of Nuada. No one ever escaped from it once it was drawn from its deadly sheath, and none could resist it."

"The unbeatable sword?" Bones asked.

"It's like the Elder Wand in Harry Potter," Maddock said.

Bones gave him a long, level look. "I'm going to pretend you didn't say that."

"Well, some people do refer to the treasures as the 'Hallows of the Tuatha,'" Isla said.

Bones smirked. "And I'm proud to have no freaking idea what that means."

Grizzly suddenly spun around, his hands on his head. "The sword in the stone, in a lake. It has to be Arthur's sword."

"It's not," Maddock and Bones said in unison.

Isla put a hand on Grizzly's arm. "I think they know something we don't." She turned a sly smile in Maddock's direction, one that didn't quite mask the suspicion in her eyes. "Sometime very soon, you're going to have to elaborate on all these mysterious comments you like to make."

"Maybe," Maddock said.

"Definitely. I can be very persuasive when I think

someone's hiding something from me."

Maddock felt the heat of Bones' stare, turned away, and strode over to kneel in front of the final treasure—the stone.

The Stone of Destiny, or Lia Fáil as Isla named it, was a rectangular block of black stone covered in script on four sides. Atop the stone, another triskele had been engraved around an onyx gem. The sharp, clear lines told him that the Celtic image had clearly been added on much later than the other script.

Maddock immediately noticed the broken corner. "This is it!" He fished into his pocket and drew out the chunk of black stone they'd recovered from the U-boat—the object that had set them on this quest. As he held it up to the broken corner, he felt a tug, as if a magnetic attraction drew the smaller stone back to the larger.

"What's up?" Bones asked.

"It's like it's trying to get back to where it came from."

"So? Let it."

Maddock reached to put the broken corner into place, but before he could affix it, it flew from his fingers, drawn by an invisible force. It snapped into place with a soft *snick*. For an instant, Maddock thought he saw a silver flickering deep in the heart of the black jewel. He stood and took a step back.

"The German spy actually made it here," Bones said. "I guess he couldn't very well take the treasures all by himself."

Maddock shrugged. "Either that, or something interfered with his plan."

"What kind of writing do you think it is?" Grizzly asked as Isla once again began clicking away with her camera.

"Some form of ancient Hebrew. Wouldn't you say, Bones?"

The big man nodded. "We've seen enough of it over the years." He paused, a look of wonderment passing over his ruddy features. "We won't know for sure until it's translated, but if the legends are true, we are looking at the stone where Jacob laid his head almost four thousand years ago."

Isla lowered her camera and moved to stand beside Maddock. A hush fell over the group as they slowly turned to gaze at the legendary treasures.

"It's real," Isla whispered. "It's all real." She took Maddock's hand and gave it a squeeze. "Even the jewels are real!"

"What do you mean?" Maddock asked.

"The treasure was often referred to as the 'Jewels of the Tuatha.' I always thought it was metaphorical, referring to how much they were prized, but each of these objects contains an actual jewel."

"I noticed that." Maddock wasn't quite sure what to make of the jewels. They might merely be ornamental, but he'd seen enough stones with odd powers to know not to take anything at face value.

"This is going to make the best documentary ever!" Grizzly took out his video camera and began recording.

Maddock turned to Isla. "You found your treasure. How does it feel?"

Isla smiled. "It's amazing. I can't even begin to describe it."

Maddock nodded. "It's why I love treasure hunting. There's no feeling quite like it. Of course, there's always the inevitable letdown once it's over. But that goes with the territory."

A strange, disturbing smile crept across Isla's face. She looked up at Maddock, a gleam in her eye

"Over? Oh, no. This is only the beginning."

"What are you talking about?"

Before she could answer, Maddock saw movement out of the corner of his eye. A glimmer of light somewhere down the passageway.

"Someone's coming."

CHAPTER 32

The Shrine of Danu

"Everybody take cover. Flashlights off," Maddock said. His order came a moment too late. Shots rang out, echoing thunderously through the cavern. One zipped past his ear as he rolled to the ground. Another pinged off the stone inches from his head.

"It's the Tuatha!" Isla hissed. "They've caught up with us."

"And it looks like they don't plan on letting us out of here alive," Bones said.

Maddock took cover behind the pedestal that supported the Stone of Destiny. Bones squeezed his bulk behind the stone block upon which the cauldron stood. He heard footsteps as Isla and Grizzly scrambled for cover.

On the other side of the lake, lights bobbed up and down—headlamps.

"You got odds, I got evens," Bones whispered.

Maddock took aim. Two shots in quick succession and the Tuatha in the lead fell back with a strangled cry. His companions scattered. Maddock and Bones each took aim and squeezed off a single shot but couldn't tell if either had hit its target.

Suddenly, the headlamps went out, blanketing them in a darkness that was unnerving in its totality. All fell silent.

Maddock wondered what the Tuatha's next move would be. The smart play would be for the enemy to simply wait out Maddock and the others. The Tuatha had them outnumbered, almost certainly outgunned, and could likely call on a wealth of reserves.

What I wouldn't give to have Willis and Matt covering our asses right now.

But if the Tuatha had intended to wait for them, why had they continued the pursuit all the way to the shrine, and thus exposing themselves to danger? They must have a reason for the urgency.

And then it hit him—they believed in the legend of the treasure, which meant…

They're afraid we'll be unbeatable if we take up the sword and spear.

No sooner had the thought passed through his mind than the Tuatha made their next move. Lights flashed on from several different angles. Bones reacted immediately, squeezing off a shot that burst one of headlamps.

Multiple bullets answered Bones' single shot, and the big man curled up behind his scant cover.

"What the hell?" he muttered. "That bullet should have gone right through someone's forehead."

"They took off their headlamps and pointed them our way. They can see us but we're going to have a hard time seeing them," Maddock said. "We could try to even the odds by shooting all of the lights out, but that will cost us precious bullets."

"Bastards." Bones suddenly rolled to his right, fired a single shot, and rolled again until he was sheltered behind the pedestal that held the spear.

Somewhere in the darkness, a voice cried, "I'm hit!"

"Let's get them!" another cried. The sound of running feet and then someone was sprinting across the stepping stones, blazing away with a handgun.

Maddock put one bullet into the man's gut. The Tuatha lurched forward and tumbled into the water. Maddock watched him sink, a dark cloud of blood billowing up through the water.

Shots continued to ring out from the semi-darkness. Maddock and Bones targeted the muzzle flashes. A couple of their bullets hit their targets. The numbers were evening out, but not the ammunition. An answering shot grazed Bones' calf.

Bones let out a curse, but waved away Maddock's questioning look.

"I've had worse," he said.

Maddock nodded. His friend's wound was minor,

but it was only a matter of time before things really got ugly. They couldn't hide from the bullets forever.

"It's like the Civil War in here," Bones said.

"How do you figure?" Maddock asked, firing his last bullet.

"We've got the fighting skills and the defensive position. They've got the weapons and the numbers."

"I'm sure a bunch of Yankees would argue with your analysis," Maddock said as Bones fired another shot. "Empty?"

Bones nodded.

"Hold your fire!" a woman's voice shouted. After a few seconds, she called out again, this time to Maddock and his company.

"You on the island. I think we need to talk."

"If you think we're giving up, you're dreaming," Bones said.

"Don't be so hasty. You're sitting ducks out there, and if you're not out of ammunition, you will be soon."

"We've still got the unbeatable spear and sword," Bones said.

The woman laughed. "As if you knew how to use them. You are unworthy."

"We found them," Maddock said. "I think that makes us worthier than you."

"One among you is worthy." Finally, the figure appeared from the darkness. It was Brigid, upon whom Maddock had spied at Culloden.

From the darkness, Maddock heard Isla let out a tiny gasp.

"I want the treasure, and I want Isla Mulheron," Brigid said. "As long as I have those things, I don't care what happens to the rest of you."

"You're not taking Isla," Maddock said.

Brigid laughed. "Take her. She'll come with me voluntarily, won't you dear?"

Maddock's retort died on his lips as Isla stood and slowly moved forward, an unreadable expression on her face.

"Isla, get down!" Maddock said. "Are you crazy? She's got at least one of her goons still active out there. Maybe more."

"She won't let them hurt me," Isla said, her voice trembling.

"You don't know that."

"Yes, I do. She's my mother."

CHAPTER 33

The Shrine of Danu

Maddock's eyes darted from Isla to Brigid and back again. He could now see the family resemblance, but still couldn't believe it. Isla had led him to believe her parents were dead.

"Mother, what is this?" Isla said. "How are you...alive?"

"It's a long, complicated story," Brigid said. "I promise I'll tell you about it when we have the time."

"But, you let me think you were dead." Her voice was cold, devoid of emotion. "How could you not tell me? And what about Father?"

"It was essential that you be kept in the dark. Isla, you have to believe me. I did it for us."

"Let's not forget, this is the woman whose people were trying to kill us just a few seconds ago," Maddock said.

"I gave strict orders that she not be harmed. As I said, I want her and the treasure."

Maddock racked his brain, trying to come up with a plan. Obviously, Brigid couldn't be trusted. Sure, she might let her own daughter leave safely. *Might.* But there was no reason for the woman to leave him, Bones, or Grizzly alive once she had what she wanted. But what could he do?

"Think we could swim for it?" Bones whispered.

Maddock shook his head. "Swim where?"

"Good point."

Brigid moved to the water's edge, casting a pleading look at her daughter.

"Meikle's been helping you, hasn't he?" Maddock asked, playing for time.

"Yes, what little help he's been. It seems Isla managed to play him like a violin," she added, a note of pride in her voice.

"Did he know all along that you were alive?" Isla asked. "Is he a part of…whatever this is?" Her sweeping gesture took in her mother, Fairly, who had risen from his hiding place and stood holding a pistol as if it were a writhing serpent, and their two surviving underlings, both of whom wore blood soaked clothing that indicated they were nursing wounds.

The odds were not yet in their favor, but there was hope. If Maddock could draw Brigid and Fairly out onto the island, maybe he and Bones could disarm them. Then it would be a fair fight.

"This is the Tuatha de Dannan," Brigid said. "Meikle is not a member, but he's been useful at times."

Isla forced a small, sad laugh. "All this secrecy, all these years lost, and for what?"

"For what?" Brigid threw up her hands. "Isla, don't you understand? It's real. It always was. The United Kingdom is falling apart. The tenuous bonds that held Scotland and England together are dissolving. Britain is losing its identity, being overwhelmed by outsiders. Anti-Irish politics is on the rise. Europe as a whole is falling apart. The Celtic people have never needed the Tuatha more than now."

Maddock frowned. Did this woman really mean this crap, or was she just trying to mesmerize Isla with a mad tale?

"Celtics?" Maddock said. "You mean the people that pretty much covered Western Europe once upon a time? You're going to wave around a sword and spear and they'll all bend the knee?"

"Most have lost their way," Brigid said, "but let me ask you this. Where is the Celtic language still spoken? Ireland, Scotland, Brittany, Wales, Cornwall. We have not forgotten. Even Brittany remembers."

"France?" Bones said. "Screw the French."

Brigid ignored him. She continued to lock eyes with Isla.

"What do you think is going to happen?" Maddock asked. "The Tuatha will rise again?"

"The spirit of the Celtic people will rise. We will unite, break free of the yolk of the English. Soon our cause will spread as others remember their true roots. They will remember who we were before the Roman church broke us."

"You think the English will stand still for that?" Maddock asked. He suddenly remembered that Isla had said something similar the night before.

"England is collapsing from within. They are torn down the middle politically. Terrorists on both sides fuel the fire. And as they fall apart, my allies are prepared to step in." She beamed at Isla. "Isla, I am part of a new family, a *sisterhood.*"

The word pierced Maddock like a dagger. He and Bones had encountered a group called the Sisterhood before. Instinct, and Brigid's emphasis on the word told him it was the same organization, and if that were the case, something had gone very wrong.

"I know this will be difficult to believe, but we are directly descended from the original Tuatha—my family and your father's. We are royalty, and one day you will be queen."

Isla's eyes widened in amazement, her features softened. "No. That can't be." The smile slowly creeping across her face suggested that, deep down, she truly believed it.

"It's true," Brigid said. "Why do you think the Tuatha was always such an important part of our family? The focus of so much of our work."

"Isla, don't believe her," Maddock said, but she clearly wasn't listening. Maddock needed to break the spell.

"You never told Isla what happened to her father," he said. "You have something to hide?"

Isla stopped short. Brigid flinched.

"He is lost to us and we have the corrupt government from which we shall break free to think for it." She held out her hand to Isla. "You completed the quest. You proved yourself worthy. Join us. Please."

"You have to let my friends go," Isla said. "They did nothing wrong. If it weren't for them, we wouldn't have recovered the treasure. Will you guarantee their safety?"

"Of course," Brigid said, but the semi-darkness could not hide the narrowing of her eyes, the forced tightness of her smile. Maddock knew she was lying.

Perhaps Grizzly realized it too, or maybe he was overcome by a momentary wave of heroism, but at that moment he leaped out from his hiding place. With a cry of, "No!" he snatched up the sacred spear and drew his arm back. "You won't take her."

Shots rang out. Grizzly uttered a low cry of pain as the impact spun him around and he fell, face-first, to the ground, clutching his shoulder. The spear clattered to the floor and rolled away until it stopped against the base of the statue of Danu.

"So much for the unbeatable weapon," Bones said.

"Scratch that legend," Maddock agreed.

Brigid had noticed, too. She frowned. "That shouldn't have..." she whispered. As quickly as it had come, the frown was gone, replaced by a cold smile. "Come with me, Isla. We'll get your friends out of here and then we'll have all the time in the world to talk."

"No!" Maddock reached for Isla, but she was already gone. He watched helplessly as she leaped out onto the stepping stones and ran to embrace her mother. He had lost her.

"Either of you guys got a bandage?" Grizzly groaned.

"Of course." Maddock rose to his feet, but before he could take one step, one of the Tuatha fired, the bullet pinging the ground inches from his toe.

"I'm just going to bandage his wound," Maddock said, hands raised. His eyes roved all around. There had to be a way out of this.

Isla and her mother had reached the shore. She whirled about at the sound of the gunshot. "You promised not to hurt them," Isla said.

"They know too much. I'm sorry." But there was no regret in Brigid's icy voice.

"But, Mother!"

"Can you honestly say they would support our cause?"

Isla didn't reply.

Maddock sensed they had seconds left. A whirlwind of thoughts spun through his mind. Should they grab the Tuatha weapons and try to fight? Could they swim for it? And what about Grizzly? Could he swim with his wounded shoulder?

And then he noticed something strange. A faint flicker deep within the crimson stone upon the spear of the Tuatha, as if the gem were coming to life. A second light, a silver shimmer, almost too faint to see, danced within the triskele carved on the floor.

It all clicked into place in his mind. The pattern carved on the floor of the chamber at Dunstaffnage. The same pattern encircling each gemstone. And here it was at Danu's feet.

"It's the triskele! Get the treasures inside it, now!"

He and Bones sprang into action as Brigid shouted, "Kill them!"

Bones shouted a question, but his words were lost in the torrent of gunfire.

Bullets sizzled through the air all around them as Maddock and Bones heaved the Stone of Destiny onto the ground at Danu's feet. Maddock immediately knew he'd made the right call. Silver light danced within the onyx jewel, and the pattern on the ground shone brighter.

"I'll get Grizzly," Bones shouted.

Maddock nodded, then turned to grab the cauldron, which he set alongside the stone. The light within the triskele grew in intensity.

"Now we're really sitting ducks," Maddock muttered. "No more darkness to hide us."

As Bones hauled Grizzly, still clutching his injured shoulder, to the center of the islet, Maddock took hold of the sword of the Tuatha and slid it free from the stone.

Holding it up before him, as if it could ward off the bullets, he stepped backward onto the triskele.

The blue stone in the pommel of the sword shone with brilliant light. Around him, the spear and cauldron added their red and golden glows; and atop the Stone of Destiny, the black gem spat flashes of silver light as the four treasures came together within the ancient Celtic symbol.

"What the hell is happening?" Bones said as the triskele suddenly burned with white light, turning the cavern bright as day.

"Grab the spear," Maddock said.

"Sure, give the spear to the Indian." Bones snatched up the ancient weapon. "Do I throw it?"

"I don't think we need to," Maddock said.

He realized that something had changed. He could see muzzle flashes as the Tuatha fired upon their position, but he could scarcely hear them. Only dull pops reached his ears now. The air around them seemed to thicken and everything slowed.

He watched, bemused, as a bullet swam toward him in slow motion. He moved to the side and it floated on past.

He turned to Bones, who had also realized what was happening. Grinning, he used the shaft of the spear to swat another of the slow-moving slugs.

"You guys look like the Flash!" Grizzly's garbled voice sounded as if it were coming from underwater.

Maddock ducked another bullet.

"Do we just keep dodging until they're out of ammo?" Bones said, his voice similarly odd and distant.

"I don't know." Maddock turned his head in time to see a bullet fired from behind them making its slow way toward Grizzly. He swatted it away and watched as it splashed into the dark water.

And then everything came rushing back to him. The thunderous sounds of gunfire. The acrid smell of gun smoke. The dampness of the cavern. Everything moved at full speed now.

Including the bullet that tore into his thigh.

Maddock looked down in disbelief as blood began to soak his leg. Had the magic gone?

Another bullet ricocheted past him. And then he realized what had happened. He'd stepped outside the triskele.

Holding the sword out in front of him, he staggered back into its protection and felt the strange, thick air envelop him. They were safe, but they couldn't remain here forever. If Brigid were smart, she'd call for reinforcements and wait them out. And unless he was badly mistaken, the woman was no fool.

Grizzly shouted something unintelligible. Maddock turned to see the cryptid hunter, holding the cauldron like a shield, pointing with his injured arm at something out in the water.

Maddock immediately saw what had caught the man's attention.

A dark shape sliced through the water. He knew right away that this was no seal. It was huge, covered in a thick, dark hide, and it left a wake like a speedboat behind it as it zipped past the islet.

The gunmen on shore were so focused on turning the cavern into a shooting gallery that they didn't see the beast until it was too late.

A serpentine neck rose from the water. In the light from the glow of the treasure, Maddock saw the creature's long, narrow head, its jaws filled with dark, razor-sharp teeth. It was magnificent and terrible.

It struck like a viper, tearing out the throat of the first Tuatha. The man reeled backward, hands clutching his ruined throat. He was already dead, but didn't know it. He wobbled, then tumbled forward into the water.

Fairly, standing close by, scarcely had time to turn and fire a wild shot before the guardian of the treasure struck. Its teeth severed his arm at the elbow, his forearm, along with the gun he held, splashed into the water. Screaming, he turned to run, but the beast lashed out with its tail, sending him flying through the air. He struck the cavern wall with a sickening thud and slid to the ground, leaving a trail of blood and gore behind him.

Maddock caught a brief glimpse of Brigid and Isla fleeing into the darkness. He couldn't believe what he was seeing.

The last remaining Tuatha, the red-haired woman called O'Brien, emptied her magazine at the beast of the lake. When it ran dry, she flung it at the creature, and then made a dash for the safety of the Shrine of Danu.

She almost made it. Reaching the last stone, she leaped, but the beast snatched her in midair. It caught her by the leg and began to whip her back and forth like a dog with a new toy. O'Brien cried out in rage and fear as the beast flung her this way and that like a rag doll.

Maddock's first inclination was to go to her aid, but then he remembered. In this situation, O'Brien was the killer, the beast the protector. At least, it was momentarily their protector.

Apparently the thought had not occurred to Grizzly. As Maddock and Bones watched the terrible scene unfold before them, the cryptid hunter, cauldron clutched in one hand, pocketknife in the other, stumbled forward.

"Grizzly, no!" Maddock reached out, snatched the cryptid hunter by the back of the shirt, and yanked him backward.

His hand soaked with the blood that oozed from his wound, Grizzly lost his grip on the cauldron. It clanged dully to the ground and rolled to the edge of the water.

The world came back into sharp focus. The air cleared. From the open water where the beast had carried her, O'Brien's screams rose in sharp, terrible pitch. Maddock's heart fell.

The cauldron had passed the edge of the triskele.

The spell had been broken.

CHAPTER 34

The Shrine of Danu

O'Brien's pained shrieks died a gurgling death along with the rest of her. With one final twist of its neck, the beast flung her torn body onto the islet. Maddock ducked as one of her arms tore free and flew past his head. He spared a glance at the shredded corpse, then turned his eyes back toward the guardian of the lake.

The beast met his gaze with its black-eyed stare. She tilted her head like a confused puppy.

Maddock felt himself relax. Perhaps she sensed that they meant her no harm. He wasn't sure why he'd suddenly decided the creature was female. It was the mental association with Nessie, he supposed.

The aquatic reptile gazed at him for a few seconds, and then she opened her mouth and let out an angry hiss.

"Take a step back, there, Maddock," Bones said.

"We need to get the cauldron back inside the circle," Maddock said, eyes locked on the beast. He took a step forward, and it hissed again.

"Maybe she won't mess with us," Grizzly offered. "She's the guardian of the treasure."

"The treasure we're now holding," Maddock said, still watching the angry creature, which swam slowly, inexorably closer to them.

"But we were protecting it, too."

The creature let out a high-pitched shriek and shot toward them.

"Try telling her that," Maddock said.

The beast struck, and Maddock did the only thing he could. He struck at her with the sword.

A flash of blue, and the creature drew back, a shallow gash across her snout. She hissed and struck again. Slowed by his injured leg, Maddock barely managed to dance out of her reach. His weak blow struck her across the back of her powerfully muscled neck. Another flash of light, but no damage that he could see.

"Looks like you're just pissing her off with that thing," Bones said. The sound of his voice drew the beast's attention. She snapped her head around to face him. "Whoa, Nessie!" Bones said. "Just chill, girl."

His words fell on deaf ears, or whatever orifices a plesiosaur used for hearing. The creature snapped at Bones, and only his lightning-fast reflexes kept the snapping jaws from closing around his throat. He ducked, and then came up fast, stabbing her throat at the vulnerable place where her head joined the neck.

It could have been a killing blow, but the beast was too quick. With a flash of blood-red light, the spear head sliced a narrow cut along her neck. The beast snapped at the spear, caught it in her jaws, but couldn't hold on. Red light danced along the blade, an electric sizzle crackling through the cavern. With a pained, angry shriek, the creature let go of the spear just as Maddock staggered forward on his injured leg, sword raised high.

For a moment, he was certain it was over. The sword flashed, gleaming blue, sweeping toward the exposed neck of the legendary beast. But his sword fell on empty air, and clanged down on solid rock in a shower of blue sparks.

"You almost killed me, Maddock!" Bones shouted.

"I was trying to save you!"

"Look out!" Grizzly cried.

Something powerful struck Maddock across the back of the thighs. His legs were swept out from under him and he hit the ground hard on his back. Pain radiated in all directions from the base of his spine. He tasted warm salty blood in his mouth.

"That hurt." He forced his eyes open to see Bones leap backward as the beast's powerful tail swept back toward him.

Somehow, Maddock managed to roll to the side. He felt the rush of foul air and the splash of dank water as the tip of the tail sliced through the air mere centimeters from his face.

"I got the cauldron back inside the symbol, but she's not stopping," Grizzly said. "Maybe she's immune to the magic."

"Either that or she's got the bloodlust in her," Bones said, fending off the creature with another thrust of the spear. "No telling how long it's been since she's tasted human flesh. This chick's got the munchies. I guess a Tuatha snack wasn't enough to satisfy her."

Maddock's eyes flashed from the beast to the cauldron in Grizzly's hands.

He had an idea. A crazy, foolish, probably doomed to fail idea, but it was the only one he had.

"Give me the cauldron." He snatched the gleaming kettle, turned and looked around. There, a few feet from him, lay O'Brien's severed arm. Grimacing, he picked up the severed limb and dropped it into the cauldron.

"Bones, keep her distracted for just a couple more seconds!"

"What the hell does it look like I'm doing?" Bones ducked behind the statue of Danu as the creature snapped at him again. She struck the statue, shattering the face of the ancient Goddess as her fangs snapped shut.

Maddock staggered to the edge of the lake, as close to the beast as he dared. He scooped some water into the pot then set the cauldron down at the edge of the triskele.

"Dinner time!" he shouted, clanging the sword against the rim of the cauldron.

He stumbled backward, barely keeping his feet. Beneath them, the Celtic pattern once again burned with a powerful intensity. Brilliant light danced within the depths of the golden gem inside the cauldron. The cauldron itself began to glow, and then, the water inside began to boil. Steam spiraled upward, spinning in strange tendrils like gossamer threads.

Despite its grisly contents, the aroma was like no scent Maddock had ever smelled. It reminded him at once of venison, good bourbon, and fresh cucumbers.

"Am I crazy, or does that smell like chocolate chip cookies?" Grizzly asked.

"Smells like the chicken wings at my strip club," Bones said.

The beast seemed to notice, too. She cocked her head and stared at the cauldron, the fight forgotten. Slowly, she lowered her head toward the bubbling liquid.

"When she starts to eat," Maddock whispered, "run!"

The beastie of the lake plunged her head into the cauldron, dipped up the steaming brew, birdlike, raised her head, and let it run down her gullet.

Maddock didn't have to tell the others what to do. Equal parts adrenaline and desperation overcame their injuries, and they ran, leaping from stepping stone to stepping stone, and back onto the ledge. As they vanished into the dark tunnel, Maddock stole a glance back to see the creature still devouring the contents of the cauldron.

"The cauldron of the Dagda, from which none came away unsatisfied," Grizzly panted as they ran. "That was brilliant!"

"Maddock gets one good idea a year," Bones said. "I just try to be somewhere close by when he does."

They emerged from the Well of the Seven Heads two hours later, much to the surprise of a confused-looking pair of nuns. One let out a shriek and the pair turned and fled.

Maddock looked down at his torn, dirty, blood-stained clothes, and thought he understood. Then he remembered he still carried the sword of the Tuatha.

"Just like Maddock to scare off the hot chicks." Bones, still holding the spear, peered over the edge of the well.

"Don't worry. I won't make a *habit* of it."

Bones narrowed his eyes. "Leave the puns to me, Maddock."

CHAPTER 35

Loch Ness

Maddock sat at a rickety picnic table outside the Boathouse Lochside Restaurant. It was a small, quaint-looking establishment, its green walls blending in with the trees that shaded its white roof. A purple sign that read *The Boathouse* hung from the wall just to the left of two tall picture windows.

Grizzly, his arm in a sling, stood nearby, chatting with an elderly couple who had recognized him from his investigative work. The cryptid hunter's words drifted over to where Maddock sat.

"I can't say for certain that I'll be studying the Loch," he said. "It's not that I don't believe in Nessie. It's just that it's been done so many times. Maybe the old girl could use a break."

Smiling wistfully, Maddock looked out across the dark waters of Loch Ness. In the distance, a boat loaded with tourists sliced through the water. Its occupants leaned on the rails, clutching cameras and smartphones, all eager for a glimpse of the legendary beast of the lake. He smiled. If they only knew the truth.

"You coming?" Bones said. "Food. Ale. Babes." He frowned. "Well, babes for me; maybe one for Grizzly if we can find a chick with low expectations."

"As opposed to the low self-esteem girls for you?" Maddock asked. He shifted around in his seat, his wounded leg throbbing.

"Don't get snippy with me, Maddock. It's not my fault your side ho joined up with some Celtic terrorists."

"I was just kidding." Maddock took out his phone. "I'll be along in a minute. I need to call your sister. She ought to be awake by now."

Bones nodded slowly. "Depending on how that conversation goes, there might be some babes inside for you, too." He reached out and put a hand on Maddock's shoulder. "I know this is weird because it's my sister, but no matter what happens, you and I will always be brothers." He snatched his hand back as if he'd touched a hot stove. "And that's the only wussy thing I'm going to say to you for the rest of the week, unless I get stupid and get into the tequila tonight."

"You realize you exist in a perpetual state of halfway to stupid, don't you?"

"Screw you, Maddock." Bones turned on his heel and headed back toward the restaurant.

Maddock hesitated, then punched up Angel's number. Her drowsy voice answered after the first ring.

"Hey, you."

"Hey, yourself."

Another of the long, uncomfortable pauses.

"You've been out of touch for a couple of days," she said. "That usually means you've been doing something interesting."

"Well, if you call almost getting eaten by the Loch Ness monster interesting, then yes."

The couple who'd been chatting with Grizzly looked sharply at him as they passed by, but kept moving.

"Don't lie to me, you assclown."

"I'm serious. We found the treasure of the Tuatha de Dannan, got attacked by their modern descendants, I got shot, and then…"

"Whoa!" Angel interrupted. "Back up! You don't just drop a bomb like that on me and keep going."

"It's not that bad," he assured her. "Besides, the monster was a lot worse than the bullets. She almost took us out."

"You didn't hurt Nessie, did you?" she asked.

"Angel, she tore a guy's throat out, turned another man to jelly, and ripped one of their partners into bite-sized snacks."

"But she didn't eat *you*, did she?"

Maddock let out a long sigh of exaggerated patience. "I managed to distract her so we could get away. She's only a little worse for the wear."

"Good. I love Nessie."

Maddock grinned. "Only because you've never met her."

Angel laughed. "What happened after all the carnage?"

"The treasures weren't the sort you can sell. Two of them we brought out and arranged for them to be delivered to the National Museum of Scotland, along with directions to the shrine where we left the other treasures. We told our contact about the monster, too, but I doubt anyone will believe him." Alban Calderwood, the professor who'd helped them in their search for the Stone of Destiny, was well-connected, and had proved useful for passing along information without naming too many names. Maddock trusted he'd do the right thing in regard to information concerning the monster.

"You didn't bring the other treasures with you?" Angel asked.

"The monster was sort of in the way. Anyway, once we crossed the Is and dotted the Ts, we had to get cleaned up and stitched up. Now we're going to drink the pain away."

Angel didn't miss the word "we," so Maddock described the injuries they had suffered and assured here they would all be fine.

She let out a long, exasperated sigh. "You and I had better never have sons. I've got enough to worry about with you and Bones."

"Are we having kids? Are we even getting married?" He probably should have handled that more smoothly but he was tired and in pain. Anyway, it was out there now, for better or worse.

Angel fell quiet.

"I've been trying to figure out how to talk to you about this. My life is changing fast."

A cold feeling hung heavy in Maddock's gut. This was the talk he'd been dreading.

"I think I've been in love with you since the first time my idiot brother brought you home for a visit. I was just a teenager and I worshiped you. And then when you said you had feelings for me, well, things went awfully fast. *I* went awfully fast, pushing you to set a date."

"What are you saying?" Maddock's voice sounded strange, distant.

"I want to figure out our new normal before we get married, and definitely before we talk about kids. Maybe take a break. Is that okay with you?"

Maddock frowned. "Are we breaking up?"

"No, you freaking asshat. I mean, that's not what I want.Let's just give each other a break." She paused. "Look, I know I've been distant, and maybe I've screwed things up between us. If it's over, you can tell me."

Maddock reached into his pocket and took out a folded sheet of paper. He'd found it stuck beneath the windshield wiper of their vehicle when they'd left the Well of the Seven Heads. He unfolded it and read, for what must have been the twentieth time, the message contained within.

Please give me a chance to explain.
Isla.

A telephone number and email address were scribbled at the bottom.

"I hear you. You're right. Let's cool things down for a bit."

Strangely, although this hadn't been what he thought he wanted, he felt relief. They talked a little while longer, more relaxed and upbeat than they had in weeks, maybe months. After they'd hung up, he made his slow, aching way into the restaurant.

Bones and Grizzly had ordered up a pitcher of ale. Grizzly pushed a mug into Maddock's hands and urged him to "catch up." Maddock grinned. The cryptid hunter would never be a friend, at least, not a close one, but he had guts and hadn't flinched in the face of danger. That had to count for something.

"To a mystery solved," Grizzly said, raising his mug. "Even if no one else ever learns the truth."

"Cheers." As he raised his mug, Maddock locked

eyes with Bones, saw his friends questioning gaze. He shrugged and forced a half-smile.

Bones seemed to understand. He took a long swig of ale, belched loudly, and set his mug back down.

"Got a question for you, Maddock."

"We're not breaking up, exactly. Just taking a break. Neither of us is in any hurry to get married."

Bones waved the reply away. "Save that for my mom and your sister. They're the ones who care about that crap. I've got a much more important question."

"And that would be?"

"What treasure are we going to hunt for next?"

Maddock grinned.

"Oh, I've got a couple of ideas."

EPILOGUE

Cornwall

Isla looked out the car window at the vast emptiness of the Cornish countryside. Rolling hills as far as the eye could see. Bodmin Moor was a lonely place—a fitting match for the way she felt. She would have welcomed any distraction from the internal struggle that tore at her heart. Had she done the right thing? Could her mother be trusted? And what was this Sisterhood of which Brigid spoke?

She had so many questions, and so far, her mother had answered precious few, always saying that the explanation was complex and would take more time than they had at the moment. Furthermore, Brigid claimed there were things she had to show Isla, people Isla needed to meet, before they began to untangle the knot. They were on their way to meet one such person.

Once again, her thoughts drifted to Dane Maddock. She could still see his eyes, blue like the sea on a stormy day, feel his embrace. She remembered their one kiss, all too brief. He had turned her away, but she had seen his reluctance, felt his desire. It was not over between them. If he was still alive.

Tears welled in her eyes. He had to have survived. He was strong and resourceful. Surely he had escaped the beast that guarded the treasure. She still couldn't quite believe the legends were true. All of it—the beast, the treasure, and its mysterious power.

"What's wrong, dear?" Genuine concern filled Brigid's voice. In so many ways, her mother was just as Isla remembered her. But the deception of the past several years, coupled with the woman's remarkable rise in station, had built a wall between them that Isla was not yet ready to break down.

"Just thinking about Dad," she lied.

"I have people working on that right now. When I

learn the name of the MI5 agent who was responsible, we will have our vengeance."

"But it won't bring Dad back," Isla said, dabbing her eyes with a tissue.

"Sometimes revenge is all we have to give. That and seeing his dream come to fruition. We will honor his memory by completing the task."

Isla remembered all the times her father had regaled her with visions of a proud nation united by the bonds of their Celtic heritage and the worship of the Tuatha de Dannan. A society healed of the sharp divisions brought about by the Roman church and the influx of adherents to other false faiths. A nation which respected the earth, as their ancestors once did. She almost smiled at the memory of his passion and devotion to his cause.

Brigid thumbed through her phone and breathed air through her teeth. "Another attack today. Five dead." She shook her head. "The children and grandchildren of Abraham. Strange that the Jews, Christians, and Muslims are cousins in faith, yet they treat one another like the bitterest of enemies."

"Strife within families surprises you?" She made no effort to soften her acerbic tone. "Have you already forgotten the Well of the Seven Heads?"

"Of course I haven't. It's simply another reminder of the death toll that can be placed at the feet of these so-called religions of love and peace. You'd see no such internal strife in a pagan nation."

Isla wasn't so sure, but she couldn't deny the carnage wrought by religious division, especially in the new century. Which side was to blame, she couldn't say. Nor could she say definitively that the pagan faith was superior. But given the track records of Christian and Muslim nations, could a nation devoted to the Tuatha de Dannan possibly be any worse?

The rolling hills gave way to a dense forest. A few minutes later, the driver slowed and turned off the main road, stopping at a security gate. They only sat there for a couple of seconds before the gate swung back and they headed up a long drive. Obviously, they were expected.

Up ahead, a medieval castle stood atop a lonely tor. The tall turrets stood stark against the gray sky. Atop the keep, a banner flapped in the wind. She didn't recognize it, but thought she could make out the shape of a dragon.

A pair of suited security men escorted them inside. After the events of recent days, Isla was keenly aware of the presence of armed men who might do her harm. Then she reminded herself that she was now on the side of those who had been chasing her. How strange life could be.

The men escorted them to a well-appointed office lined with lush carpet and decorated with antique furniture.

"She'll be with you in a moment," one of the guards said. "Please make yourselves at home."

Brigid took a seat on a chair in front of a large desk. Isla wandered the room, examining the artwork. At first glance, one painting looked like a family portrait, but the three women in the picture looked nothing alike. One was a blue-eyed blonde, the second raven-haired, while the third had green eyes and coppery tresses.

A second painting caught her eye. It was a version of "Le Morte D'Arthur" by James Archer, but with some differences. The artist had added to the top and bottom so that it filled a door-sized frame. Odd, but interesting.

Finally, she wandered over to the picture window behind the desk and looked out onto the grounds below. A small formal garden lay just beneath them. At its edge lay the forest that surrounded them. As she gazed out, she caught sight of something colorful soar through the treetops and disappear from sight. She frowned. It had only been the briefest of glimpses, not even a second, but what she had seen was no bird.

Behind her, she heard a click like a latch being opened. She turned to see the "Le Morte D'Arthur" painting slide to the side. A tall, blonde woman, striking in her beauty, stepped through.

"I apologize for keeping you waiting," she said.

"We only just arrived," Brigid replied smoothly.

"Please have a seat," the woman said to Isla, motioning to the chair next to Brigid.

Isla sat down, and the blonde woman took a seat on the other side of the desk. There was something about this woman, this place... She felt like she ought to know both.

"Welcome to Modron," the woman said. "Your mother has told me a great deal about you, and I've read some of your pieces. You are not only a talented writer, but you clearly have a sharp mind, keen analytical skills, and a strong sense of determination. I respect that."

"Thank you," Isla said, still struggling to grasp at the threads she was certain she could weave together. It was like the feeling of having a song title on the tip of her tongue, but just out of reach.

"Are you well?" the woman asked.

"Forgive me, but I'm certain I ought to know you." And then it all came together. Cornwall, Bodmin Moor, Modron, and a woman named Morgan.

"I thought you were dead," she blurted.

The woman held up a hand and smiled patiently. "You are thinking of my sister. She was called Morgan, and she is indeed dead."

"What are you called?"

The woman smiled. "You may call me Nineve. It is not my birth name, but I have claimed it as my own."

Isla frowned. According to legend, Nineve was a pagan enchantress and one of the Ladies of the Lake.

"I thought your family lost control of this estate when your, I mean, her plot to assassinate the royal family was foiled."

"We did, temporarily. But our roots are deep, and we have branched out more widely than any ever suspected. With the aid of some new allies, I have reclaimed our family estate, taken my sister's title for my own, and exacted revenge against her so-called sisters." Her eyes flitted to the portrait on the wall. "And now it is time to form a new sisterhood."

"Forgive me, but I was under the impression that your sister sought to bring all of Britain beneath her heel. That includes Scotland."

"I told you she was a sharp one," Brigid said.

"That was her plan…our family's plan," Nineve said, "but I would be content with England and Wales. Overall, our aims are not so different."

"And those are?" Isla asked.

"Unity through acceptance of the old ways, and peace through strength."

Isla nodded. "And how do you expect to achieve those aims?"

"The same as you—with power. Political, social, and most of all, ancient powers that defy modern understanding, and will capture the imaginations of the masses."

"And do you possess anything that fits that description, or are you hoping to share in our power?"

Nineve quirked an eyebrow. "My sister found several such treasures, but they were lost due to the actions of other members of the Sisterhood. I have managed to recover the most important of those items. As to your power, the last I heard, you did not possess any of the treasures of the Tuatha."

"That will be addressed in short order," Brigid said, tersely. "My people have already retrieved the Stone of Destiny and the Cauldron of Dagda, as well as the Urquhart Treasure."

"And what of the spear and sword?" Nineve asked.

"They will soon be in our possession. Dane Maddock was foolish enough to turn it over to the national museum, as if we don't own enough staff members there to take whatever we want."

Nineve sat up straight. "Did you say 'Dane Maddock'?"

"He helped me find the treasures." Isla's heart beat out a rhythmic tattoo. How could this woman possibly know of Maddock? Had he been involved in the hunt for the treasures of which she spoke?

Nineve rose from her chair, turned to the window, and laced her fingers behind her back. She stared out at the forest for ten anxious seconds before turning around to face them.

"Well, then," she said, rubbing her hands together. "It appears we have a great deal to discuss."

END

ABOUT THE AUTHOR

David Wood is the author of the popular action-adventure series, The Dane Maddock Adventures, and many other works. Under his David Debord pen name he is the author of the Absent Gods fantasy series. When not writing, he hosts the Wood on Words podcast and co-hosts the Authorcast podcast. David and his family live in Santa Fe, New Mexico. Visit him online at http://www.davidwoodweb.com.

Made in the USA
San Bernardino, CA
08 August 2017